CW01636113

GODDESS OF AIR

KINGDOM OF FAIRYTALES: PETER PAN BOOK 4

ANNE STRYKER

J A ARMITAGE

Edited By Rose Lipscomb

Cover by Enchanted Quill Press

Proof Reader: Tina Merritt

❀ Created with Vellum

KINGDOM OF FAIRYTALES

You all know the fairytales, the stories that always have the happy ending. But what happens after all those storybook characters get what they wanted? Is it really a happily ever after?

In this prequel, you will find out what happens next, be transported back to those lands you fell in love with and be prepared to meet some new characters along the way.

Kingdom of Fairytales is a new way of reading with one chapter a day and one book a week throughout the year beginning January 1st

Lighting-fast reads you won't be able to put down

Read in real time as each chapter follows a day in the life of a character throughout the entire year, with each bite-sized episode representing a week in the life of our hero.

Each character's story wrapped up at the end of every season with a brand new character and story featured in each season.

Fantasy has never been so epic!

READING ORDER

Kingdom of Fairytales is a 52 book series split into thirteen seasons. Each season has a four book story arc of a fairytale character with the last season seeing them all coming together. You can read any series first with the exception of thirteen, however it is recommended that you read in the order below…

PREQUEL

SLEEPING BEAUTY

1. Queen of Dragons
2. Heiress of Embers
3. Throne of Fury
4. Goddess of Flames

LITTLE MERMAID

5. Queen of Mermaids
6. Heiress of the Sea

7. Throne of Change
8. Goddess of Water

RED RIDING HOOD
9. King of Wolves
10. Heir of the Curse
11. Throne of Night
12. God of Shifters

RAPUNZEL
13. King of Devotion
14. Heir of Thorns
15. Throne of Enchantment
16. God of Loyalty

RUMPELSTILTSKIN
17. Queen of Unicorns
18. Heiress of Gold
19. Throne of Sacrifice
20. Goddess of Loss

BEAUTY AND THE BEAST
21. King of Beasts
22. Heir of Beauty
23. Throne of Betrayal
24. God of Illusion

ALADDIN
25. Queen of the Sun
26. Heiress of Shadows
27. Throne of the Phoenix

28. Goddess of Fire

CINDERELLA

29. Queen of Song
30. Heiress of Melody
31. Throne of Symphony
32. Goddess of Harmony

ALICE IN WONDERLAND

33. Queen of Clockwork
34. Heiress of Delusion
35. Throne of Cards
36. Goddess of Hearts

WIZARD OF OZ

37. King of Traitors
38. Heir of Fugitives
39. Throne of Emeralds
40. God of Storms

SNOW WHITE

41. Queen of Reflections
42. Heiress of Mirrors
43. Throne of Wands
44. Goddess of Magic

PETER PAN

45. Queen of Skies
46. Heiress of Stars
47. Throne of Feathers
48. Goddess of Air

KINGDOM
OF
FAIRYTALES
URBIS PRISON
SHIPLEY
THE VALE
AZREN
BADALAH
DESERT
KISBU
DRACONIS
ZHORE
ELDER
MOSA
ABORIA
URBIS
AZURE
ENCHANTIA
EMERALD CITY
OZ
SKYLA
FLORIS
TULIS
THE FORGE
ARCADIA
RENAIS
MELFALL
ATLANTICE
ANTLA
W
E
S

25TH NOVEMBER

Sunlight touched my cheeks, waking me from my bed of moss. I blinked, unable to remember when I'd fallen asleep. Last night was fuzzy. I recalled reaching the Nixies and greeting their leader before they led us to the pile of moss I now rested on. An eerie song filled the air.

I felt as rested as I had when I'd woken in the sirens' garden, and I lifted my arm to find the bandages, and my wounds were gone. Whatever laced the air around creatures like the Nixies and the sirens had healed me again, fortunately. I would need my strength, and so would Bay.

Sitting up, I peered around. The glimmering pools of water remained where they had been, every weeping tree's branches skimming the reflective surfaces in a light breeze. Calm as it seemed, something ominous lurked. My heart thumped.

Bay and Whisper. They weren't in sight.

"Worry not." A voice rose from one puddle orifice,

and a Nixie followed, the same from the night before, I think. But it was difficult to tell. They all looked so similar with large, regal foreheads, scaly green and blue skin, and glowing eyes. "Your friends have gone on ahead."

Ahead? Ahead where?

Nerves bundled in my stomach as I glanced at the golden temple. In the sunlight, it looked even more imposing. At night, gleaming with silver and swallowed by darkness, it hadn't appeared quite as large. Now, just looking at it directly was blinding.

"Why didn't they wait for me?" I asked, throat tight.

"It would not have mattered. They must face their nightmares alone for now, though only you must succeed alone."

"Wow. Thanks," Skye droned, and I jumped, finding him hovering beside the Nixie, arms folded. She looked at him, meeting his nasty frown. "Am I or am I not going with her?"

The Nixie's lips pursed, and some spattering of knowledge flashed through her eyes before she smiled. It was a moist, dreadful thing. "Yes, well. You will see what I mean."

He flinched, flitting to my side and standing on my shoulder. "I'm not sure we want to…"

Her laughter was like a bubbling brook, soft and cheerful, but a film closed over her eyes when she blinked, and a chill shot down my spine. "I agree with Skye."

"You have done this before." She tilted her head, and her wet hair slapped against her cheek like seaweed. "These temples were erected by the first natives with a magic more powerful than what this world or yours remember. The souls of any who have stepped foot within linger in fractals, ready to test the next guest. You will face your own mind in a quest each of you must overcome if you are to make it out alive with the answers you seek."

"It relies on all of us?" Air stuck in my chest.

"Yes," she said, "but mostly you, Lyric."

"No pressure," Skye mumbled.

I was feeling all the pressure. I was a demigod who didn't know how to use my powers, tasked with saving my home and then the world. And I was staring at a quest that my friends had already started and could perish from unless I somehow passed.

Why couldn't they have waited? We could have talked about this more, maybe found a way around taking more chances with our lives. I shook my head. No, I had to stay strong. The Nixies had protected us through the night and healed me. The woman before me, though unsettling in appearance, didn't appear unsettled by the fact that Hook and whoever else the Enchantress had gathered to her side would have fewer people to stand in their way if we failed. If I trusted these powerful creatures and they trusted me, could I trust that meant everything would be all right?

"Don't overthink it, child." Her brows knitted delicately, and for the moment, she appeared less monstrous. "You may enter the temple when you are ready, but realize the longer you wait, the longer your friends must face their demons."

She had said nothing about demons. Skye stiffened, shifting uncomfortably. We looked at each other, and worry darkened his blue gaze, but he didn't press me. He only nodded, offering his support.

I leaned on that, took a deep breath, and nodded, standing. "Let's get this over with..."

"You mean to say you are ready?"

"As I'll ever be..."

She laughed again, but this time other voices joined in her mirth. They pooled together until the sound was akin to the rush of a waterfall. "That is simply not true, but you are on your way. You have all you need, and that will be enough." She extended a webbed hand toward the temple entrance, and I squinted against the sun at the pit of darkness she expected me to enter.

It was not a gradual descent into the pitch. I stepped forward, stopping before the wall, and lifted my hand. It disappeared into the blackness, and my breath held. The second I entered fully, I wouldn't be able to turn back.

"We've done this before," Skye murmured near my ear, but his hold on my hair tightened.

"You have to promise not to leave me like last time."

He stayed silent a moment, and my heart pounded with every second he delayed. At last, he whispered, "If the Nixies are hinting at what I suspect, I don't believe I'll have a choice. However, for as long as I can, I'll stay with you."

That was as good as I was going to get. Glancing back at the Nixies one last time, I met the woman's glowing eyes, shoved down a shiver, and stepped into the temple. A blinding light consumed me whole.

. . .

Night curled around me in an unusual way. Like I was a part of it. I stood firmly, but my feet were not visibly on the ground. I checked for Skye and found him still perched on my shoulder. His tiny presence calmed me enough to take in the rest of the dream-like surroundings.

Home. It was home. Peter's tree stretched before me in the forest, the same limbs and plateau I had grown up in yawning into the sky. Pixies darted around like they didn't see me at all, like this was a normal night for them. I swallowed, waiting for the twist, the moment when everything changed, the moment when what I loved disappeared before me, and then an impossible task presented itself.

That hadn't happened in the first temple. But that temple hadn't ripped me away into a vision the second I stepped inside either.

Everything stopped. The pixies halted as one and peered at each other with wide eyes. Their voices were questioning, but my ears only picked up bells. "Do you understand them?" I asked Skye.

"Understand who?" His brows lowered.

"The—" My heart skipped. A baby. The soft wails of a child cut through the trees, and from the corner of my eye, a form appeared garbed in a cloak. My heart rate picked up when I caught a snatch of orange hair peeking out of the bundle in the woman's arms. Me. That was me. And if that was me, and this was here, then...

Desperate for a glance of my mother, I tried to fight through whatever held my feet on a solid plane, but my body remained suspended in the air, feet firmly planted against the barrier.

"Lyric,"—Skye's voice pitched—"what is it? What's going on?"

"It's my mother and me and my home. You can't see it?"

"I'm seeing something completely different," he replied but didn't elaborate. Only a touch of anxiety tainted his tone, but he gripped my hair tighter, and his heels pressed into my shoulder.

Any question I was going to ask Skye died when the woman lifted her hand and knocked on the tree. Every second waiting was torture. This was the moment she left me, abandoned me, decided I wasn't worth keeping, and that a twelve-year-old would be good enough to raise me.

Who was she? How dare she?

Peter peeked out of the secret entrance and lifted a brow. His eyes narrowed, and something inaudible mumbled past his lips.

I hoped, and I prayed that the woman would hesitate, kiss my cheek, show that she didn't want to give me up, but when Peter stopped speaking, she held me away from her body without reservation. He floated over me, disgust scrunching his nose. The woman, my mother, said something, and his eyes widened. His head shook. He reeled back.

By now, the other lost boys were fighting at the secret entrance for a glimpse of what was going on. My eyes were filled with tears.

Peter looked horrified when the woman urged him to take me. His head shook again, and his arms folded.

Tinkerbell zipped out of his hat, hovered over me, and then laughed, disregarding me. Both of them nodded their dismissal and turned to leave.

A tear fell, a sob wracking my chest, and I covered my mouth.

"Hey, Lyric, what's going on over there?" Skye asked.

This had to be a lie, I reasoned. Peter *had* taken me. This was just a matter of the temple getting into my head. Nothing more. Peter would walk away here, and I'd have to confirm it was a lie. What a simple, insipid little test. "I'm fine," I choked. "It's stupid. Are you okay?"

"Well enough," he mumbled, and even I could hear the lie amidst my clogged head, but neither of us addressed it further.

I waited for the scene to end. It didn't. Peter's retreat stopped, and he looked over his shoulder, listening to unheard words my mother spoke. His eyes narrowed, but he faced her again, peering at me. I continued to cry, both presently and in the scene.

Peter stuck his finger in his ear and toyed with whatever she had said. When she offered me to him again, he sighed, glanced at the Lost Boys, then took me into his arms. A tiny frown marred his lips, and he held me like I was something filthy, but my gold-rimmed eyes opened, the deep brown meeting his, and the expression drifted away into something of surprise.

Baby me sniffed, and my wails ceased when Peter poked my forehead.

A deep sigh filled his chest like I was a burden he couldn't care less about, but he said some final thing to my mother, then turned back toward home. She turned away as well, and I watched her, waiting.

She didn't so much as slouch.

The scene dropped out of my sight, and I blinked at a long cave tunnel lined with glowing moss. At least, it looked like moss, but it breathed. The whole of the stretching path before me swelled and deflated with breaths like I was standing within a living creature, and panic filled my chest.

Peter hadn't wanted me.

The thought entered my mind when the creature surrounding me inhaled. It left with my shuddering exhale. My lips trembled as they parted.

Peter hadn't wanted me.

He had taken me, but he hadn't wanted me either. Only whatever my mother had told him convinced him I was worth the trouble.

"Skye?" I choked, squeezing my eyes shut.

"Yeah…?" Torment filled his soft voice, but he was here; he was still here.

"What do you see now?"

It took him a second, but he mumbled, "Creepy cave."

"Glowing, mossy walls?"

He half-scoffed. "That's not moss, but sure."

"Well, at least we're in the same place now," I snapped, not needing the reaffirmation that the walls were indeed not harmless moss. "I just saw my mother abandon me with an unwilling Peter. So that's nice."

"Peter's twelve, Lyric. He's stuck in an eternal cootie phase. Of course, he wasn't thrilled to be handed a baby girl, but the point stands that he kept you when he could have given you to any number of people on Skyla." He tugged on my hair, and I winced. "Don't let this place get in your head, Daughter of Pan."

Daughter of Pan. I hadn't heard that for so long.

He's right. Peter kept me. *Because of what my mother told him that made him take me?* I opened my eyes and glared at the tunnel. I would have shaken my head if it wouldn't have sent Skye flying. *Skye was right,* I confirmed again, harsher. *Besides, it doesn't matter now; Peter's forgotten you.* The new thought sliced a deeper gash, and I swallowed, blurting, "What did you see, Skye?"

"Bay."

The vague answer led to a rush of annoyed thoughts. Just as well since they pushed out the darker ones.

"Let's get moving," he said.

"We're going deeper into this thing?" I tensed, eyeing the monster.

He sighed. "What else can we do?"

I glanced behind me, immediately wishing I hadn't. At my back, the moss closed off wherever we'd come from, and it was closer than I'd ever want to be to the breathing walls. At least, solid ground rested beneath my feet, but when I blinked, it turned neon in a flash, softening like flesh. I blinked again, and it returned to stone. "I don't like this. What the hell is this?" I wrapped my arms around my chest and stepped forward to move away from the back wall.

"You can't trust anything in here, Lyric. Remember that."

That's right. Thank goodness he was here with me. I don't know how I'd be able to do this on my own.

Taking a deep breath, I walked forward, grounding myself in the light weight on my shoulder.

Of course. The grim thoughts bubbled to the forefront of my mind. *The Nixies knew you wouldn't be able to handle this alone.*

"Airwoman," I breathed, talking myself through it, "the voices are incessant."

He hummed in agreement, and I gnawed my lip, glancing at him. His eyes were dull, and his lips rested in a firm line. Worry ate away at my gut.

"More specifically, what did you see?" I asked.

His gaze found mine for a moment, then it drifted away. "I saw what they did to him. That's all."

The pirates. Bay's torture. Sickness tightened my stomach. "What angle are the voices taking with that?" Somewhere in my heart, I knew I shouldn't pry, but talking kept my mind off my own demons. At least, until my thoughts wandered. *Demons. That's what the Nixie said Whisper and Bay were facing. Demons just like this. And I had to save them somehow. I didn't even know if I could save myself.*

"They're saying I wasn't there for him. They're blaming you for that, trying to make me leave you alone in this. But I won't." His brows furrowed, and I didn't mind the pull on my hair. "Sure, I wasn't there for him then because he told me to make sure you were safe, but I could have refused. More than that, I don't have to take responsibility for what *they* did. I know the real enemy. I can't be turned against myself or my friends." He offered me a weak smile that was the strongest thing I knew in that moment. "Pixies are pretty loyal little assholes, aren't we?"

Despite myself and my terrifying surroundings, I smiled back at him, my soul feeling a little lighter. "They sure are."

The second the last word left my mouth, he disappeared.

My soul jerked out of my skin. "Skye?" I called into the darkness. Nothing responded.

You're alone.

The walls breathed. I stood in the belly of some magical beast, alone. Alone with my thoughts. They screamed in my head, reminding me how little I had accomplished in my life, how everything up until this point had been wasted time. There wasn't a single thing worth mentioning.

I was utterly worthless.

Just a sad little girl who wanted to explore the world, a sad little girl who had nearly died dozens of times on her first adventure.

No wonder Peter didn't let you leave Skyla. He knew better than to send you to your death.

"Shut up," I hissed, moving forward. The ground jerked beneath me, and a lump caught in my throat. The ground was the same living substance as the walls. "This isn't real." Skye had said so. I believed in him. *This wasn't real.*

This is magic. Anything is possible. Even if it isn't "real," it can definitely still kill you.

The words in my head were far more potent than the ones I forced past my lips. This place had taken my final lifeline away. And the Nixies had known. I couldn't trust my thoughts. I couldn't trust myself at all.

"But what if," I murmured, forcing myself to stumble

over the rocking terrain, “they aren’t your thoughts. What if something else is in your head, and it’s not you.”

“On the contrary,” the collection of voices I faintly remembered from the last temple brushed past my ear like a soft breeze. They collected into a glowing form, then they took my shape. “I am you.”

The temple beast took a deep breath, and wind howled through the expanding walls.

“These thoughts are bred from your mind. At one point or another, they’ve belonged to you. Aren’t they pitiful? And aren’t you?” The glowing reflection sneered and looked away like I disgusted her. And didn’t I? Myself, I mean. Didn’t I disgust myself?

According to the sirens, I was some great piece in a bigger plan, but I couldn’t even find it in myself to embrace the idea of that.

“How do you expect to believe in yourself when no one else does? Your oldest friend,” my reflection winced and looked truly pained, “Whisper…she didn’t even believe in you enough to fly. And Bay? He sent a pixie to babysit you the second you were separated.”

The walls closed in, tighter than they were before. I could hardly breathe.

Was Skye still here, just invisible? Was he watching me crumble? Was he regretting believing in me to save him and Bay and Whisper?

Picturing his frustration frustrated me, and my fists clenched. “I said, shut up!”

“Pathetic.”

“That isn’t shutting up.” I gritted my teeth and glared at myself. She looked more like me now. Orange bled into her hair, and brown swirled in her eyes. Her despondent eyes. Another monstrous inhale. Another whip of air. My hair flew before my face, and I realized that hers was a dirtier shade. Her eyes were a duller mud.

She was every mediocre idea I had of myself. No gold touched her irises because I didn't believe I was special like that. Her hair was thin and bland because I didn't believe I had any right to stand out, to look even a fraction like Peter. Unwanted, she slouched.

I hated her.

The walls constricted further, but only I seemed to notice.

"Might as well end up swallowed here," I spat. My other looked at me, and I narrowed my eyes at her. "Is that it? I thought it. I said it. But I don't believe it. I *can't*. My friends need me."

"Since when have our friends ever needed us?"

"No," I growled, and the creature froze, the mossy walls still for the moment. "*My* friends. The Nixie said they would need me, so I'm not going to let this be where my adventure ends."

"Must you always rely on someone else?"

I unfolded my arms and took a step toward her. "So what if I rely on others?"

"It's pathetic."

"No, it's not." Those words resonated in my heart, resounded in my head, and I felt them swell in my chest. "It's strength. The ability to believe in others isn't easy. It's so much safer to build walls and stay inside them. I may be wrong about someone. I may trust something that I shouldn't. I've done that countless times since coming to Neverland. When you rely on someone, you allow them access to your foundation. They may rip the ground out from under you." I thought of Bay, Hook's son. "They may not be who you thought they were at all."

"It's stupid then," she hissed.

I smirked. "Yeah? So?"

She didn't miss a beat. "You're an idiot."

Scoffing, I lifted my chin and said, "I prefer 'pretty loyal little asshole.'"

The form's features broke, shattering my likeness and morphing into something else. "Can you do nothing on your own?" it shrieked. "Can you not even find your own words to say?"

The fleshy walls snapped to life, roiling, and the ground beneath my feet jerked with them. I lost my footing and fell. My stomach lurched. Air whipped against my face as I plummeted into a pit of darkness. Untouched by whatever gravity yanked me, the form remained standing before me, unmoved, a howling wraith of a creature.

I grasped at thin air, finding nothing to hold onto. There was nothing. All around us, pitch black, and yet I could see myself and the figure clearly. None of this was real. But again, it was magic. And magic could kill.

"No one is here to save you!" the figure screamed, a harsh wind scratching through its throat.

I squeezed my eyes shut, hoping the jumping feeling in my stomach would vanish if I blocked the sight. It didn't. It continued to accelerate, leaving my gut behind. If only Skye were here. I could fly if he were here.

I can fly even if he isn't.

The thought came unbidden, and I wondered if it

was me or some force in this place. Who here would encourage me when so far everything had tried to break me down? I swallowed, but a thought hit me.

Even if we were separated, I wasn't in here alone. I was never alone. If I was going to believe in Skye, in Whisper, in Bay, in everyone, then maybe I should start listening to what they had to say.

Whisper said I could save the world.

Skye said I could create tornados.

Bay said he loved me.

I swallowed, tears burning in my eyes and dashing away in the torrent of wind as I fell. "You're wrong!" I yelled. "Everyone is here to save me. Everyone I've believed in, relied on, trusted, they live in me. Maybe I'm not strong enough to believe in myself effortlessly like Whisper and Bay can. Maybe I have to find a convoluted way to do it. But maybe, just maybe, that's okay." I flattened myself against the wind, slowing my descent. "This is who I am." I threw out one arm. "And I am loved." I threw out the other. "And I am enough."

My body became what it was fighting against. Lighter than air. No dust on my skin. I flew. It may have been a magic-induced dream, but I decided not to believe that thought. This was within me. It was natural, like flying always had been. It was real. Something powerful skated beneath my skin, making me aware of every breeze, every breath. The blackness surrounding me and the form before me weren't real at all.

Air was. It was everywhere. And I felt it in every empty space. Exhaling, I caught sensations of solid walls, chambers, long halls. Inhaling, I recognized a gentle breath nearby. Skye hadn't gone anywhere after all.

I looked over the amalgamation before me as it shuffled through a dozen forms, grasping the fragments of past souls who had dared to step foot here. Whisper and Bay blinked by before it was me again. But the not-quite-me. Dull hair. Bland eyes. Weak and afraid.

I floated in the black space, staring at her. There were so many flaws. So many doubts. But that didn't make her worthless. That didn't make me worthless.

"I accept you," I said. "We are enough."

When I blinked again, the blackness had disappeared. Before me, was a temple chamber outlined with eerie blue torches. I looked down to find my feet above the ground and grinned. I lifted one leg, then the other, and pressed my lips together to hold back my smile. A tingle of pixie dust wasn't anywhere to be found. This was *me.*

All those years I'd spent collecting something I already had within me… If only I'd known sooner. The feather marks on my arm burned with purpose. They *were* from my wings; I had always been able to fly.

Skye groaned, and I found him hovering beside me, his face twisted with twinges of discomfort. He blinked out of something unseen and set a hand against his face. "Why do these places have to hate people…?" His eyes widened after he squinted at my dangling feet. "What the… But I haven't…"

I landed softly. "I think I figured some part of this demigod thing out."

He blew a laugh out his nose. "Atta girl. So we can

get the hell through this now?" He returned to my shoulder, sitting this time and rubbing his temple.

"As quickly as possible." I lifted off the ground, skimming forward down the tunnel path, embracing the sensation of magic-fueled weightlessness. "Have I ever told you that you curse an awful lot for 'darling incarnate'?"

He scoffed. "Who says darling incarnate doesn't curse?"

After several minutes—or hours—of flying, the scene before me changed in a blink. I was somewhere else. Somewhere I hadn't ever been before. My brows furrowed, and I put up my guard, keeping from touching anything.

"Are you with me?" I asked Skye.

"Yep." He glanced over the flowering fields with similar apprehension. It was so bright. I knew we had to have walked into either Whisper's or Bay's nightmare, but whose nightmare would be so...

A swarm of brilliantly colored butterflies filled the air as a girl ran through the flowers. Her dark skin and bouncing hair told me exactly who it was, but she was far younger than she had been for a long time, and only panic filled her eyes.

"No!" she screeched.

My immediate instinct was to make sure nothing chased her, but Skye tugged on my hair and pointed the other direction. Walking away, but somehow moving faster than she could run, was her father. Tears streamed down her cheeks, her little arm outstretched.

She tripped, smashing face-first into the plants. She curled in on herself there and didn't bother to get up.

I blinked, and the whole scene rewound.

Butterflies burst off every painted petal. "Papa!" She fell, sobbing.

And again.

Butterflies. "Please!" She collapsed. Her tiny arms covered her head, and wracking breaths filled her chest. I had never seen her like this concerning her father. By the time I found out what had happened, she only smiled sadly and said that sometimes that was how the tide was: giving and taking without emotion.

My heart ached for the little girl lying in the grass, and determination lit a fire in my stomach. I had to break the cycle. This time when the world reset, I floated to the spot where she always tripped. She ran toward me, staring directly through me, her plea on her lips. "Don't leave!" Her foot snagged on something invisible, but this time, I caught her.

The pleasant meadow broke with an ear-splitting crash. Stone walls replaced the flowers, the blue sky, and the hundreds of butterflies. We stood in a tiny, towering room of thick grey, only the ceiling open to display a starry night. Whisper, her correct age now, sobbed, gasped, and realized things had changed.

Darting away from me, she took in her surroundings, then steeled, wiping her cheeks. They were splotched beneath her red eyes. "I'm sick and tired of this," she hissed. "Let me out of here already."

I opened my mouth to tell her that's exactly what I planned to do, though I wasn't exactly sure how, but her voice replied behind me, "No. This is where we're safe."

I turned, coming face-to-face with a pristine Whisper. A cold, hardness held her brown eyes in a state of unshakeable charm. The real Whisper huffed, folding her arms and facing the wall, trying to find a place to grasp; the fake Whisper took the moment her back was turned to glare at me.

Whisper grumbled, "I'm not safe in here. I have to get through this, find the answers we need about the Fountain, and get back to Lyric."

"Lyric?" her other questioned, her voice lilting with humor. "Sweet, sweet, little Lyly? She's practically helpless without you, isn't she?"

"Hush your ugly face," Whisper snapped, but my heart had already clenched. Were those her real inner thoughts? Was that how this worked?

"What an,"the other chuckled—"interesting insult to choose, all things considered."

Damn. I swallowed, watching the other Whisper sashay to her side and drape herself against the wall. *Whisper's inner voice was sassy as shit.*

"Back to Lyly," the other glanced my way, "you really have to protect her, don't you?"

"Of course! I mean, she is younger than me." Whisper gripped the stone, and I realized her fingers were bloody.

"Yes, well, not by too much, though you'd think there were eons between you."

Whisper planted her feet against the wall, managing to hold on. "So she's a little immature. Like I'm any different; all I want to do is marry my 'moth prince,' whom I call *'moth prince.'*"

"At least, you know better when it comes to important things." The other checked her prim nails. "I mean, she knew that Bay kid a week before running off with him to airwoman knew where. He's Hook's son. He might be using us to get to the Fountain. Pirates are conniving like Mom has said. I wouldn't put any faith in a single one of them."

Whisper sucked in a breath as her grip faltered, and she skidded back to the ground. "Listen," she spat, "you aren't going to get in my head about my friends. Lyric is Lyric. I love her to death, no matter what you say."

"I never said we didn't love her. Just that sometimes she can be a bit of an ignorant child."

Whisper bared her teeth and growled. "She fell in *love*. That's a thing that happens, and it can be blinding."

Her other set a finger against her cheek and pursed her lips. "Yes, right, you never would have been pushed off Skyla at your birthday party had you not been blinded by your own little *love*."

Whisper's chest pumped. "There, see? Who saved me then? Lyric and Bay."

"And if they hadn't?" Her other's delicate brows dipped. "We can't let our guard down like that in case they decide not to next time; there can't be a next time. We already know that the people we're supposed to trust the most fall through when it matters the most."

"Can I hit you?" Whisper raised her fist. "Are you real enough to hit? I'm not normally an aggressive person, but I feel like I'm allowed to give myself a beating when I'm talking crap."

"Is that really what she thinks of us?" I asked, my throat tight. How exactly was I supposed to step in? She couldn't see me.

"Maybe they are things she's thought of, but that doesn't mean that they resonate as truth." Skye looked at me. "This place preys on our cracks. Whatever it can use, it will. Sometimes passing thoughts appear when we don't want them to. Recognizing the lies is important to overcoming them."

My resolve hardened. "How do I reach her?"

Her other tittered. "Should we go back to our memories? Which time someone has failed us is our favorite?"

"I don't want to hear it. I don't want to see it. And I *definitely* don't want to relive any more of it. I don't care if it's dangerous out there. I know it's dangerous out there."

Her other threw out her hands. "Then why are you trying to leave? I'm trying to keep you safe."

"I'm strong enough to keep myself safe!" Whisper yelled, facing herself, tears gathering in her eyes. "I'll get out of this by myself and deal with whatever happens because of that choice by myself as well."

"You don't have to deal with anything by yourself!" I blurted.

"Lyric—" Skye started, but I stepped in front of Whisper, ignoring him.

She stared through me, but I didn't care. Maybe if I spoke enough, she'd be able to hear me. "All these years, we've been by each other. And sure, maybe I've failed you a lot, maybe I'm not as mature or smart or confident, but no matter what, we've promised. Again and again. *We will never be apart.*"

Whisper blinked, two crystal tears slipping down

her cheeks. Surprise touched her expression, and she lifted a hand to her face.

"Lyric's going to save the world. She's destined to." Her other exhaled, bored. "After that, she'll be strong enough to go on the adventures she's always dreamed of. You'll become a memory in her life just like you've become one in your father's." She flicked her gaze up, smiling brightly. "A pleasant memory, of course. We're wonderful."

"Lyric is going to save the world," Whisper said. "I believe that. I believe in her."

Her other unleashed a booming laugh. "Oh, really? No, you don't! You can't even trust that she'll make it back from her little Skyla adventures when you've asked her to help you plan something!"

"That makes me horrible then, not her!"

Her other's smile was nasty and cruel. "I never said she was horrible."

Whisper swallowed and turned back to the wall. She lifted her bloody hands. "Just go away. You're annoying me."

"I am you." Her other sighed, leaning against the wall.

"No, she's not." I reached for Whisper, but she stepped away from me, searching the fortress for another handhold. My fists clenched. "How am I supposed to do this if she can't hear me or see me?"

A scraping noise made me jump away from the walls. They inched closer together, and my stomach flipped. The other Whisper smiled calmly and continued to check her nails.

"Not again," Whisper murmured, swallowing. Fear

filled her eyes, and she gnawed her cheek, controlling her breaths as she placed her hands on the grey stone and tried to lift herself once more. Her moccasins skidded, and she couldn't catch herself this time, falling flat on her rump. Wincing, she held her bleeding hands against her chest.

"Maybe you don't want to leave after all."

Whisper sneered at herself, but she remained seated on the ground, cradling her bloody palms close to her body.

"She's not going to do this alone." I looked at the walls, then lifted my hands. Something hit me, and my eyes widened. Air surrounded us. I could find myself as a part of it. I floated off the ground, and a buzz of magic lit beneath my skin. Holding onto that sensation, I wrapped my hands around the wind and sent it sailing toward Whisper.

Her hair whipped across her face and over her shoulders. She turned her head and tried to tame her locks, but she still didn't see me.

"Maybe you can lift her out of this place?" Skye mused.

"My thoughts exactly." I took a deeper breath and let it out as I clenched my fists.

The wind harshened, creating an updraft that tore at her clothes. Panic filled her gaze, and she scrambled away from the gusts. "What is this? What are you playing at now?"

Her other merely shrugged.

I cut the wind off and drew back, shaking my head. "I don't have that much control, and I won't risk hurting her."

"Don't doubt yourself now." Skye flitted off my shoulder. "The only way we reach Bay is if we figure this out."

I pressed my lips together and lifted my hands again before promptly dropping them. "No. This can't be right. It's all a test, and this isn't my test; it's hers. Before, in the other temple, the only way I got through was when I decided I would trust myself over what that thing told me. This time, I had to accept myself and believe in my own power." Realization hit me hard and cold. My feet touched the ground again. "Neverland. It's your home, the birthplace of pixies, creatures of belief. Everything here tests belief. The changelings and pirates try to shake your trust. The sirens and Nixies don't appear safe to trust, but you have to believe in them because they hold the secrets." I recalled Peter and Wendy. A child and a bright-eyed dreamer. All the pirates. Why did pirates end up in this place? Because they dreamed of something more? Because they believed in impossible things like treasure and ruling the seas? Because, at heart, they were confident explorers who believed in themselves? They believed in themselves to the point of destruction. Peter and Wendy believed in everything. "Only children and dreamers can find and master Neverland because children and dreamers have something in common. They either violently trust others or themselves. Whisper has never had a problem trusting herself." I looked at Skye. "She needs to trust us."

Skye's face twisted, and he threw up his arms. "How? She can't see us!"

I flicked my wrist, calling a swirl of wind to spin

around her, teasing her hair upward. "Maybe not. But our efforts aren't completely invisible. In the end, this is her test."

Whisper narrowed her gaze at the sky, searching for something, some answer to my breeze, and I nodded at Skye. He huffed, skeptical, but circled above Whisper, showering her in dust. She blinked furiously when it fell into her eyes and tried to rub it away.

I caught her hands before she could.

"I love you." I smiled. "You know that. You don't have to do this alone."

Skye returned to my shoulder as I lifted off the ground, still holding her hands, whether she could feel my touch or not.

"It won't work." Her other slinked off the wall, and Whisper's gaze shot up to it. "You know that. You can't fly on your own."

"You're not alone." I squeezed her hands.

Whisper's fists clenched as she met her other's eyes. "What makes you think I'm alone?"

The woman who wasn't quite Whisper smirked. "Look around. It would take an awful lot of belief to assume otherwise."

The creature's words pounded into my skull, and I whipped my gaze to her. She winked, and everything changed in that moment. *These beings weren't our enemy.* They were us. Us and those before us. Neverland's spirit. *They wanted us to succeed.* I called on the air around us, curling it in a hug that pulled Whisper off the ground for the first second.

"I believe Lyric's right here then!" Whisper laughed. "We have never been apart." Tears pooled in her eyes, and she extended her pinky, bowing her head forward. I linked my finger around hers, noting the moment when my wind ceased, and she remained airborne beside me.

"Well, I'll be damned," Skye murmured, his blue eyes wide.

"More darling language?" I snickered.

He grumbled, "It happens when I'm stressed."

By all appearances, we rose out of the fortress, though when I checked the air, we hadn't moved but a foot off the ground. As Whisper's other disappeared below us in the vision, I watched her shift forms. For a split second, it was Bay. Then in the last instant before the vision disappeared, Peter grinned up at me, folded his arms, and nodded me onward.

My eyes closed; emotion choked me.

Whisper's gasp yanked me from the moment, and her arms crushed me against her body. "Oh, my airwoman! You were here!" She looked down and squealed. "And I'm *flying*!" Her gaze went huge. "And that was you making freak wind!" Excitement bubbled around her, something physical in the air, until her smile fell away, a little at a time. "How long have you been listening to…everything?"

My head shook even as my chest pinched. "It doesn't matter. Trust me, I said far worse things about myself."

"I believe that." Her attention drifted down the hall lit with blue flame. It seemed to go on for an eternity, and both directions looked identical. "I suppose we have to find Bay next…?"

I nodded.

She winced, gnawing her lip. "If I'm honest, I don't trust him." She looked at Skye, and her brow furrowed.

"I don't actually trust you either. I'm a thousand percent sure I'm only flying because of Lyly right now."

"It's nice that you're bringing down your walls, but do you really have to insult me to my face like that?" Skye rolled his eyes, hardly sounding perturbed.

Whisper smiled. "Yep, still can't understand him."

"The Nixies implied we all made it out together, and besides," I pursed my lips and met her gaze, "Bay isn't like his father."

I wonder about that.

The words slithered into my head, chilling my blood, and in the next instant, Whisper and Skye were gone. The scene had changed completely, and I was alone on the edge of something…something terrifying and magical.

It was a grove. And there was a fountain.

26TH NOVEMBER

Light gleamed off the pool of water, winking into my eyes, and I had to squint to make out the rivulets shooting from the center in rainbow arcs. Trees curled their bows over the fountain, blocking out a would-be sky with foliage and dangling moss.

So enclosed, I wondered where the light came from, but I didn't have much time to find it.

"Wind Song." The words came breathless behind me, and I turned to face Bay. "You're here."

He strode to me, cupped my cheek, and kissed me. Any relief at seeing him vanished in that moment. My heart thundered within my chest, and creatures exploded in my stomach. Heat bloomed on my cheeks, and where his hand found my waist, his touch scathed me. When he pulled away, I was almost too shocked to notice how tired he looked or how battered he was.

Blood smudged his cheeks and his hands and his clothes. My heart rate picked up. "Are you okay?"

"I'm fine." He smiled, glancing over my shoulder at the glimmering water. "I can't believe all this time it's been here. I waited for you; I thought we should do this together."

Magic pulsed in the air, and my brows bent. This couldn't be the real Fountain; the water of the real Fountain was gold. I peered around for Bay's other, but no one else stood in the grove. Unrest made me tense. "What happened? What have I missed?" Something was wrong because something had to be wrong. That was the point of a trial.

"A skirmish or two. It's fine. I knew there'd be trouble." He shrugged easily despite the blood all over him. I examined him closer, and my stomach went sick. *He wasn't injured.*

It wasn't his blood.

"Bay…" My throat closed, and my gaze fell on his sheath. It was hooked on his belt, and blood dripped through the laced leather. "What did you do?"

He quirked a brow at me, then looked himself over. "Oh. Right." He ruffled his hair, having the nerve to appear embarrassed. "Yeah, I know it looks bad, but none of it is real. The temple guardians aren't real. I've done this before; we both have, remember?" He touched my hand with his bloody fingers, but I didn't feel the stickiness, and none left a trail. "See?"

"You killed your other…?"

"If you'd met him, you'd have killed him too." Bay laughed, but there was something deeper in the sound, and it died far too quickly. His shadowed eyes recalled whatever dark words had been said, or maybe they still spilled into his skull. He shook either or both free. "I knew you'd make it. Should we wait for Whispering Meadow?"

Whisper had vanished along with Skye. My chest was panicking right now, but I checked the air for them. No breath disrupted the space, though, as I'd guessed, we were in a room. This wasn't real. "Whisper and Skye aren't in the temple anymore."

His brows rose. "Really? I suppose it decided only we would take care of this, then." He faced the fountain and sighed. "Look at it. Isn't it perfect? All this time, and now, finally, I have what I need to save my mother." His hand found mine, and my heart leaped when he smiled at me. It was purely joyful. How was I supposed to tell him it was all a lie? That we still had work to do?

What was the test? How was I supposed to help?

My gaze shifted over the edges, searching for any shadows, any hints of danger, but my eyes continued to be drawn back to the blazing water. Bay pulled me along with his stride, approaching the glittering pool, and my anxiety raced. I clutched his hand and shook my head. "It's not real, Bay. I don't think we should go near it."

"Don't be silly." Anger sparked in his eyes, and his hand gripped mine tighter. "Do you know how hard I've fought to get here? It has to be real. Why bother protecting something fake?"

"Believe me, Bay. It isn't real. We have to figure out the trial, then we'll be able to find where the real Fountain is."

His hand slipped out of mine, and he narrowed his eyes. "Of course," he said darkly, "it's all been too simple. You aren't real either, are you?"

I stepped back when his fingers found the hilt of his blade. "Bay..." The gleam in his eye. I had seen it before. On Hook's face. When I was Wendy. "No," I breathed, and my exhale shook.

"Prove it. Don't stand in my way. If it's not real, we have nothing to lose." He faced the pond. "But if it is..." His head dropped, and he scrubbed a hand over his face, leaving a trail of blood that he ignored. "You're a demigod, Wind Song. I don't know how a goddess's ancient blood permeates you. What if time takes me away from you?" He turned to me, lifting his tortured gaze. "I love you. If you care for me even a fraction of how much I care for you, I don't want to slip away. I refuse to leave you alone like my mother left me."

You were slipping away. Time was taking you away from me.

What choice did I have!

"You don't have to do this," I choked. Hook's face overlapped Bay's, and I stepped back, terrified of how realistic it looked. The temple was toying with my vision again. I knew that, but the meaning behind it sank deep into my soul. "You don't have to choose this."

He sighed, a joking, pained smile lifting his lips. "Is that how you're going to reject me then? By implying you'd like to watch me die?"

Airwoman. Would that really happen? Tears sprang to my eyes, but the sirens had warned me not to let him drink from the Fountain. They had told me why Peter was the way he was. I couldn't bear to watch Bay—or anyone else I loved—die, but we didn't know what any of our futures held, and watching him become like Peter...wouldn't that hurt far worse?

"I see," he murmured after I hadn't replied. Turning, he stepped toward the fountain.

I jerked after him, catching his wrist. "Don't!" This was why the sirens showed me his parents' past. They were warning me that history would repeat itself. I couldn't lose him like this. I didn't want to watch him die. I didn't want to live forever. I wanted to go on adventures with him. Grow old together. Watch our kids raise their kids. "Don't do this. This is *exactly* what your father did. I don't want to see this again. Please, Bay!"

He whirled on me, sneering. "So you are just another part of this damn temple. I should have known they'd use you against me as well." His blade flew for my throat, and I slammed my eyes shut, knowing that sharp weapon was real.

Cold metal didn't reach me.

A force burst to life between Bay and me, wrenching my hand off his. When I dared to open my eyes, his other stood between us, but unlike Whisper's and mine, his other was a precise copy. "Stop," his other said, nothing wavering in his voice. "We love her. I won't let you hurt her." One of the being's hands squeezed mine while the other held Bay's sword, refusing to let it move. Its gaze narrowed as Bay wrestled with his weapon. "Bay Darling," he said after a moment. "You have failed."

The world washed black.

"It's okay." Bay's voice called me from the darkness, and blue lights lit in the tunnel. I peered around us, then at our joined hands. He wasn't the real Bay. He wasn't there at all. Though his chest rose and fell with breath, the air around him remained undisturbed.

His expression gentled, and he repeated, "It's okay."

"It's not," I choked. "It's really not. This place brings out the deepest parts of people. *That* was Bay? I don't want to believe that!"

Bay's other cupped my cheek, offering me a half-smile. It looked so real, and I had to remind myself I had already passed my test, and this amalgamation wasn't my enemy. I squeezed his hand for strength, and it kissed my forehead. "It has been so long since I've felt this way. You and your friends have brought me fresh love." His smile became too gentle. "Thank you for it. I've already released the pixie and Whispering Meadow. I will show you where the Fountain is, then I will send you back to your friends."

"What about Bay?"

Sorrow touched the being's eyes. His hazel eyes. Bay's hazel eyes flecked with gold. "He failed. Most violently. Only the pirates who dare to enter a temple decide to cut their way through us. He has displayed greed and hatred. We cannot free him again."

"Again?" My breath caught. The last temple. He said he'd done this before.

His other nodded. "We knew you'd need him to survive this far, but now, you have Whispering Meadow and your own strength. We allowed him another chance for your sake, but we cannot risk another Peter, a cruel Peter." The being morphed, and fiery hair burned on his head. He grinned, the likeness cutting me to my core. "I was special. All of Neverland knew it. I was special, like you, Lyric. We can hear the pixies. We are fearless."

"Bay can hear the pixies! And I'm not fearless! I'm actually terrified right now. You can't keep him." Panic swelled in my voice, but the being didn't appear troubled by it.

"To be fearless isn't to be without fear."

"I'm certain that is *exactly* what it is," I hissed, still clutching Peter's hand like a lifeline. To hear his voice and see him like this, after so long, when I knew he'd likely already dismissed me from his mind. This might be the last time. That also terrified me.

"To be fearless is to not let fear hold you back. You have come this far."

"By relying on others."

Peter's brows lowered. "We have been through this; you are enough."

"Don't take him from me. I love him." The words left my throat raw, and I closed my eyes. "I love him. Give him another chance."

"We know we love him." My voice. My eyes snapped open, and my other stood there, holding my own hand, torment reflecting in my own eyes. "But another chance would be too great a risk."

"He isn't his father."

"He followed the exact path his father did. For greed, masked by love, he justified horrible things."

"He knew it wasn't real. That's the only reason he did what he did. If he..." A thought occurred to me, and I raised my head, staring my other directly in the eye. "How much control do you have over the mind of someone in your walls?"

Her head tilted, and she was Whisper's cocky other. She smiled. "These minds are ours. We do not take them because we are built from love. From the first, we were erected as a sanctuary of belief and love." Her eyes widened, and I felt fingers caressing my thoughts. "And if he fails this?"

"I will stay with him here until he succeeds."

Her head reeled back. "You can't change someone, and you don't have time to wait for him to choose to change himself."

"Then, if he fails, change time in this place. I'm not leaving without him."

Whisper's eyes narrowed, and she lifted a perfectly manicured hand. "I won't accept that." Her grin bared. "Fine. I will paint this picture you have in your mind, but you may not help him, and if he fails…I will take the memory of him from you. Your destiny is too important to be held here. How strong is your belief now?"

I trembled but took a breath. I believed in Bay. He wasn't his father. If he thought it was real, he wouldn't carve his way through in the name of his greed. "Strong enough."

Whisper sighed, smiling kindly, almost like my real friend would. "See, Lyly? This is fearless."

With those words, she, and the tunnel, disappeared, replaced by a cavern with a single entrance. Behind me, a dry fountain sat in the center of the plateau. Light rained through cracks in the ceiling. I stood before the tiered fountain, no longer myself.

Dark skin encased my small body, white robes hung to my bare feet. I felt my hair and found it silver. Something weighed against my back, and I looked over my shoulder to see wings. I was a young siren. And I was not alone in my head.

We have been here before you, child.

Or perhaps after.

Time is as it must be, confusing.

"You knew," I whispered, keeping my gaze on the only entrance, waiting for Bay.

We have always known.

And that's why they warned me.

"Finally," Bay's voice reached me from the entrance. "We finally made it, Skye."

"Let's get this over with." Skye zipped in before Bay, met my gaze, nodded, and zipped back to his side beyond where I could see. "Lyric and Whisper are counting on us to bring the power of the fountain back to them in Skyla *before* Hook attacks."

"We won't fail them. Or Mom." Bay appeared at the entrance, awe in his eyes. "I've never felt magic like this before. We're here."

"Welcome," I said, raising my arms. My voice throbbed with the voices of those before me, and my heart raced in my chest. "Welcome, Bay Darling."

His brows rose when he met my gaze, and he looked me over, glancing behind me at the empty fountain.

"I have been waiting for you." Though I couldn't see my smile, I knew it was as chilling as the sirens'. "My sisters have guided you to this moment. We are sorry to keep you from this for so long, but for the sake of the world…"

His lips parted. "You… You don't mean they've known all this time where the Fountain was?"

I closed my eyes. "We see everything. The war. The pain. The suffering. The answer."

"I don't understand. Why keep this from me? I've been looking for years! My mother—"

I raised my hand, cringing internally when I saw the pain in his eyes. "The price of this power is one of blood and sacrifice, our Bay. It appears only for a short time after that price is met. Only now, when you must use it to save the world, may we allow you access."

"Blood and sacrifice?" He approached me, crouching to my height. "What do you mean?"

My gentle Bay. "I have known my fate from the moment I was born. Please, don't worry. You must take this power with you and for yourself, or everyone will perish."

Horror filled his eyes, but he didn't move away. "You aren't saying..."

"I am."

He shook his head, rising. "No. Peter Pan wouldn't have done this. You can't be telling me the truth."

Wendy's memories of the world in her time flooded me, and I saw the words to say. "Peter Pan did what he had to in ages past, in a time when war also brewed over the land. We needed him to be our hero then. Now it is your turn."

"Lyric won't be able to fend off the pirates for long unless we do something. She needs the fountain's magic." Skye's fists clenched. "Would any sacrifice work?"

"Any precious life," I said, repeating what the voices echoed for me to say.

Skye pressed a hand against his chest and looked at Bay. "Then let me."

"No," Bay growled. "What do you think I'm going to

do without you? I can't fly without you. I wouldn't even be able to get the water to her."

There were other pixies still on Neverland. My brows furrowed, and I almost spoke, but Skye's own voice murmured in my skull, *Bay can't fly using any dust. Only mine. He only trusts me.*

Bay winced, pacing and running his fingers through his hair. His short braid came undone, and he cursed as the tie fell, before glancing at me again.

I smiled, though my heart hammered. "It is all right. I am a small price to pay for the world. I have already seen what I may miss."

"That doesn't matter," he spat. Anger boiled in his expression. "Your sisters, your family, how can I possibly take you from them? I know what that does to someone."

"But Lyric—" Skye began.

Bay snatched a dagger off his belt and flipped it in his hand. "Yeah. I know. She needs this."

"What are you—" I bit my tongue when the voices hissed at me. A siren would have no question.

Bay didn't seem to notice as he positioned the blade at his chest. "Make sure it gets to both her and my mother, Skye." His gaze flicked to me. "Tell your sisters thanks for everything."

Panic welled in my heart as he closed his eyes and—

All breath left my body when everything disappeared except for Bay. Frozen in place, he stood, his empty hands positioned before his chest. The spirit of the temple stood before him, its faces shifting constantly. "So," they said, "this is the path he has found." A sigh breathed through them, and they turned, smiling at me.

I looked myself over and found I had returned to normal. Steeling myself, I met its gaze. "He passed. I told you."

"Yes, he is capable. But such dramatics don't surround the real Fountain. It is only hidden. When found, he must not drink it. Hook, once, was like Bay. The years on Neverland have made him what he is now. Bay's core is still good, but his father's blood runs through him. He would not wear the time well either."

"What are you saying?" The words burned in my mouth.

"Some die heroes. Others become villains."

"Bay's not like that!"

The being approached and cupped my cheek. It sent a chill through me. "Your belief is a virtue; it may just be enough. Peter was young; he avoided the venomous effects of the Fountain when he took it in ignorance because he was innocent. The true terror of everlasting life through the Fountain is that the power eats away at you, again and again. What it would leave behind for those out of their innocence is nothing short of monstrous. We would all be like that."

"I won't let him drink it then." I swallowed.

"You must be certain." They nodded. "The Fountain rests on Skyla, just beneath your nose. You will not need its power. Allow Bay only what he requires for his mother, then destroy it."

"How?" I asked.

"All wind that rises must fall." They lifted their hand, and a vial appeared as they morphed into the eldest siren. The gentle woman's voice did not match her grave expression. "This. Only this. You must be certain." She clamped it against my palm, and I looked over her shoulder at Bay.

He remained frozen, his eyes closed and his hands at his chest. "How do I explain what happened here?"

"You will not have to." She released the vial and flicked her wrist. Bay vanished. "He failed. He will not remember anything past that. It has been important for him to know his failure and you to know his redemption."

The being morphed again, this time into the youngest sister. She smiled. "Protect our Bay. Good luck."

When I blinked, I stood at the temple exit. The Nixies turned as one to face me from their puddles, their eyes all aglow in the night, and my stomach clenched. Darkness swallowed the cove in evening. *How long had we been in there...?*

"Lyly!" Whisper came from the air, slamming into me with a hug that nearly knocked me back into the temple. Involuntarily, I called a rush of air to me, pushing me back to safety. It didn't get past her, and she gasped. "Did you just freak wind?"

Outside the temple, it felt more real. I lifted off the ground, effortlessly, without dust, and grinned. "I think I did."

"Ah! This is incredible!" She laughed, squeezing me.

"Did you get the location?" No joy touched that voice.

My heart skipped, and I looked at Bay. Skye hovered near him, his eyes downcast until he glanced at Whisper. Silently, the pixie provided her fresh dust, then returned dutifully to Bay's side. Shadows bled in the corners of Bay's usually bright eyes, and I winced, nodding. "I have an idea where the Fountain is, but we can only take this much." Lifting the vial still in my hand, I held Bay's gaze. "It's just enough for Wendy. No more. No less. Then we have to destroy it."

"What?" His brows shot high, and I was glad he appeared surprised more than angry. "Won't you need its power to save the world?"

I shook my head. "Worse things will happen if we don't do as the temple spirits said. Promise me, you three." I divided my attention between Bay, Skye, and Whisper, only so it wouldn't seem like I was calling him out.

Confusion muddled Whisper's face. "Of course. I don't have any use for the Fountain anyway. I'd rather not Peter-ify myself, thank you."

Some stray thought flickered in Bay's gaze, but he ran his fingers through his loose hair and nodded. "If that's what you were told…"

"It was." I landed, suddenly exhausted, and slipped the vial into my satchel. The bed of moss we had slept on the night before called to me, and I offered Whisper half a smile before I passed Bay, heading for it. "I think we should rest now. Tomorrow, we meet up with Tiger Lily, then we're heading home."

27TH NOVEMBER

"Wind Song." My heart responded immediately when Bay's voice hit me, but I didn't face him. The sun rose above the trees in the cove, showering me in a golden light. A soft breeze touched my skin, and I breathed it in.

Ocean brine.

A hint of magic.

Bay floated to my side, concern filling his eyes. His lips parted, but he looked away before words came out. "I'm sorry."

Heat crept up my neck. "For what?"

"I failed in the temple. That..." He rubbed his jaw. "It was really you in there, wasn't it? I almost—"

"It's all right." I laced my fingers together and tried to remember he had passed in the end. It wasn't easier. All I could see was a dagger plunging for his heart. "There's no way you could have known for sure."

"Still, I was so blinded by what I wanted. I thought it made so much sense. The only places in Neverland I haven't picked apart are the temples. For the longest time, I've had a hunch that the Fountain was in one, but I grew up surrounded by lore of how dangerous they were. I was too scared to enter."

"Until you met Peter's daughter and thought if Neverland loved him so much, you'd be safe if you brought her along." The clearer things became with him, the less I wanted to know. There were so many lies and plots. Why couldn't we have just stayed in his tree-house, talking about silly adventures?

"I'm sorry. My mom, she..." His voice cracked, and I glanced at him. He had brought a leg to his chest. His hair fell like a curtain over his face, blocking it from view. "She's the only family I have left other than Skye. You know what happened."

"I know a lot." A lot more than I wanted to. "And I understand. You were desperate."

"Yeah." He exhaled, and the air from his breath shook. "For the longest time, I've been living for her. Now, she's not all I have anymore. I used to only be able to see my life up until the point she woke up. Now, I can imagine something after that." He didn't look at me. "I meant what I said in the temple, and what I did."

The kiss. How had I forgotten? But then that was a silly question. It had happened right before he tried to kill me, which happened right before he tried to kill himself.

My fingers brushed my lips, and the heat at my neck crawled across my cheeks. "I like you, Bay. But..."

His fist clenched. "I never should have faced the test like I did. I was just so blinded by my preconceived notion the Fountain was within reach. I shouldn't have kissed you either. I don't regret it, but I wasn't in my right mind. I just... What they showed me... What I told myself... I've spent so many years hating my father for what he's done, worrying that I'm exactly like him. It was too much. So much that I caved and did exactly what he would have." A gentle breeze caressed his cheek, pulling his hair away from a face awash in torment. The torment eased with surprise, and he glanced at me.

My lips pressed together. "Sorry. I didn't mean to do that. I couldn't help it."

He smiled, though pain still rested in his eyes. "You're amazing, Wind Song, and I hope you know that I'm glad you found my treehouse."

A laugh escaped me. "That seems a world away."

"It is." Voice soft, his murmur drifted through the weeping trees around us and toward a horizon I couldn't make out past them.

I swallowed, feeling a lump form in my throat. Why did it have to hurt like this? I didn't know what I was supposed to do. Yesterday was a whirlwind, and now I stood on the brink of a war? A war where Skyla was only the beginning. What if I failed?

I couldn't afford to fail.

Bay tucked my hair behind my ear and smiled, half-shrugging when I looked back at him. "I couldn't help myself."

He hovered, inches away, and my heart ached. My fingers begged to touch him. Before I knew it, they had. They slipped through his hair, hesitating only when I recalled what had happened to his hair tie, the moment it had fallen in the temple.

"What's wrong?" he asked, his voice little more than a whisper.

What was wrong? This? He was Hook's son. He had proven himself better than his pirate father in the end, but the spirit had assured me darkness remained a seed within him. I shouldn't— I shouldn't, and yet...I wanted to believe. Mouth dry, I said, "I'm scared."

He swallowed, his body going rigid. "Of me?"

"No." My hand slid out of his hair and found his chest. His heart beat, racing mine. I wasn't scared of him, and maybe that scared me a little bit too. I believed in him like Wendy had once believed in Hook, and now look where she was... I was terrified of being wrong because I desperately wanted this. "You're almost out of dust, Star Boy."

He traced the feathers running down my arm. "A pity, some of us don't have wings."

In that moment, everything was him. My breath stilted, and I fought the pounding beats of my heart that brought me closer and closer to an edge I couldn't return from. Did it matter if I fell? I had never been afraid of falling, even before I knew I could fly without pixie dust.

My hand clamped in his shirt and yanked, drawing his lips to mine. He kissed me, and I melted into his arms. *Please don't be wrong.* I clutched him tight, unwilling to let go. He was air. He was ocean. He was endless.

When we parted, we didn't separate. I rested my head against his shoulder, still clutching his shirt, allowing his scent to hold me along with his arms. He squeezed me close, as desperate as he had been in his kitchen so many days ago when I'd first called him my friend. He was more than that now, though I wasn't exactly sure when it had happened. "I love you, too," I said.

His breath shuddered, and his lips touched my neck as he buried his face against my shoulder. In his embrace, it was easy to hope. It was easy to believe. This couldn't be wrong; it couldn't fall apart. A cold sort of determination took refuge in my chest.

As long as I could, I wouldn't let it.

Bidding the Nixie Cove goodbye, we picked our way silently through the treetops, deciding that flying on a clear day would only allow the pirates to know where we were if they searched, and if we took the land route, they could be lying in wait.

Somewhere in the middle, then, Whisper had said, landing on a branch and setting her hands at her hips. I'm not sure she'd left the air since she regained her ability to fly.

Skye made himself busy flitting between the two of them, and exhaustion filled him every time he collapsed on Bay's shoulder, face down against the clothes.

"Are you okay?" Bay murmured, but I heard him. He poked Skye's cheek.

The tiny creature mumbled against the cloth, "Of course, I love being hunted by pirates and having to monitor two people so they don't fall out of trees. Can someone please tell her that the dust is for if she needs it and not for doing tricks?"

Whisper skipped from one branch to the next,

hardly touching even the sturdiest limbs. Her face was so bright. Bay saw it too, and he pouted. "But she looks so happy."

"I see how it is." Skye pushed himself up, fluttering indignantly. "You'd rather let your girlfriend's friend be happy than let your pixie rest. How the loyalty has shifted. I trusted you."

Bay caught my eye then, and I looked away like I hadn't been watching the whole exchange. I had no helpful input to provide. I hadn't so much as touched a branch for the last ten minutes.

Bay floated to me, drifting at my side, and Skye groaned, falling face-first against his shoulder again. Bay's hand skimmed mine, inciting butterflies in my stomach. "Being nosy again, Wind Song?"

My cheeks flushed.

"What do you propose we do to fix this problem?" he asked.

I glanced at Whisper, who cheerfully tapped her way over the awkward terrain, oblivious. It was nice to see her so at peace after so many days of seeing restrained tension in her limbs. "She should have her own pixie."

Skye scoffed, glaring at me. "*Pardon*? People don't just 'have' pixies. We only cling to people who can understand us."

"Wendy couldn't understand you."

He rolled his eyes. "No, duh. I was never meant to be 'hers.'"

My brows rose. From even before Bay was born, Skye knew? Or had he been told? Who knew what the sirens manipulated. One problem at a time, I supposed. "Then where's my pixie?"

"Maybe none of them like you because you think we're something to be owned?"

Bay snickered, glancing away.

I narrowed my eyes at him and addressed Skye. "You know that's not what I mean. And what use would I actually have to 'own' a pixie now?"

"Um. Your friend." He rolled his eyes. "Or have we forgotten what we were talking about."

"Sometimes, you're unbearable." I huffed.

He gave me a tight smile, flitted back over to Whisper, and replenished her dust before I could get another word in.

But he definitely was a loyal little asshole.

Shaking my head, I smiled. Bay's fingers brushed mine again, then slipped around them. I looked at our joined hands before meeting his gaze quizzically.

He shrugged. "The pixie has spoken. You're my girlfriend now."

"Is that how relationships work?" I couldn't hold back my smile or blush.

His brows shot high, and a flush coated his cheeks as he glanced away. "Don't look at me. I wouldn't know either. Remember, you're the first girl I ever went to a party with. The closest thing I've had to a girlfriend before that was a girl who was a friend, and also that one's mother, so..." He pointed at Whisper, who had stopped up ahead and was hyper-focused on our joined hands. A wide smile consumed her face.

"Oh, great. She's noticed." I bit back my smile. "Play it cool."

"Have I missed something, Lyly?" she asked when we reached her.

"Of course, you have," Skye snipped, throwing up his hands and collapsing on Bay's head. "You've been high on pixie dust ever since you left that damn temple. It's a wonder you aren't hallucinating!"

"Translation?" Whisper's brow quirked.

Bay and I looked at each other, then he said, "He's kind of worn out and would appreciate you using your dust sparingly."

The innocent darling breathed curses into Bay's hair.

Whisper wasn't having the diversion. She waggled a finger between us. "What happened here."

"He kissed me," I answered.

Bay countered, "And then she kissed me."

"And we got a pixie's blessing."

"So here we are."

Whisper pressed her fingers against her lips, squealed, then jumped us both with a hug. "It happened! I thought it would happen, but now that it's happened, it's so much more than I'd hoped! The children of sworn enemies… A demigod and a pirate. Star-crossed love."

"Fitting, isn't it, Star Boy?" I smiled, but Bay's grin had fallen into something softer.

"I'm not really a pirate. More of an explorer or adventure seeker."

Or a Lost Boy. In that moment, something in his eyes reminded me of the Lost Boys. I had once asked Peter where they had come from. He said he didn't quite remember. All he knew was that, at one point or another, they had gotten lost and decided it was better to be lost together.

My hand squeezed his. “Bay was raised beside your mother for a time, Whisper.”

She turned, looking at the sky. The sun reclined on the horizon, not quite painting it in shades of dusk. “Speaking of my mother, we should almost be at our camp.”

Nixies around the meadow. “Maybe thirty minutes more?”

Bay tensed. “Should we stop for dinner first?”

“We can have dinner together. We’ll probably need it before we head back to Skyla. We shouldn’t waste time.” Whisper held her arms out, balancing as she walked across a branch. “I’m kind of worried about what they did to her. When you saw her, did she look okay?” Worry pitched in her tone, though she tried to hide it well.

He was crushing my fingers now, but his expression remained calm and distant. “I said before, they have a certain respect for each other. I don’t think Hook would hurt my childhood friend.”

“It didn’t stop him from killing all her people.” Whisper moved on before we had a chance to say anything in response. What could we say anyway? She was right.

It was easy to see what she had told herself in the temple clung. Hopefully, that would pass when we were all safe again.

I started to follow her, but Bay held me back. “Wind Song,” he whispered, his voice raw.

“What is it?”

Skye jolted up suddenly, spun to face Whisper, and

groaned. Darting, he showered her in a fresh coat of dust, leaving us alone.

My chest tightened, making it hard to breathe. "What's wrong?"

"I don't actually know, for sure, whether or not Hook released Tiger Lily."

Ice washed over my skin. "What?"

"I never saw her," he confessed.

A sinking sensation overcame me, sending my heart to my toes. I could only repeat stupidly, "What?"

"If she isn't where Whisper thinks she would be, then—"

I stared at him, my eyes wide, my heart still, dread filling every inch of my body. Mouth dry, my mind grasped for what exactly he was telling me. He had lied to us. And if she wasn't safe… "Then Hook still has her and could be in Skyla right now, with enchantress magic and a hostage." I choked, tearing my hand out of his and floating back. I covered my mouth, trying to control my suddenly panicked breaths. "Why are you only telling me this now?"

"Skye told me what the sirens said. We didn't have time to make sure she was okay. I trust they wouldn't have said what they did unless she would be safe, but we couldn't take any chances." He held his hands out, pleading, but I could hardly look at him.

I shook my head in disbelief. "How could you?"

His jaw tightened. "We couldn't risk failing. The sirens said—clearly, which is rare—if we didn't go directly to the Nixie Cove, we wouldn't succeed."

Anger exploded in my skull, hot and red. I glanced at Whisper, who danced onward with Skye, likely believing we were back here having a "moment" that she shouldn't disturb. Even when she didn't trust him, she wouldn't interrupt if it made me happy. *Airwoman.* How could I have been so stupid? Hook could already be in Skyla; he could have already confronted Peter, failed to get what he wanted, and killed her. Leaning forward, I hissed, "You better hope Tiger Lily is at their camp, Bay. In fact, you better pray."

With that, I flew to my friend, ignored my cracking heart, and left him behind.

The silence did not bode well. With darkness rising over the meager, deserted camp, everything appeared eerie and forsaken. I held my breath, praying to the airwoman, to whatever deity had birthed me, that Tiger Lily would appear.

An untouched fire pit rested beside a simple lean-to, any past ashes already stolen by the wind. Tucked in a corner of the forest with high brush, footsteps would hardly be noticeable, but something would have been disturbed had anyone been here in the past few days.

"Maybe they found her again?" Bay's voice had the decency to be choked.

Whisper stood beside me, staring blankly at the tiny camp. "She should be here. She said if we got separated, we'd meet back here…"

"Whisper…" I reached for her.

She shook my hand off her shoulder. "No! I trusted your trust in him, but my mother isn't here! We shouldn't have left the bay without her!"

"No, we shouldn't have." I faced Bay, bitterness on my tongue.

He started, "The sirens said—"

"I don't care!" A torrent of wind ripped through the space, and the lean-to collapsed. "Why didn't you tell us the truth sooner than now? If we had known, we could have left for Skyla yesterday! Every day we wait, we don't know what's happening over there; we don't know if—"

"Hook could have released her." He swept back his hair and had the gall to defend himself. "I just wasn't sure."

A sour laugh sputtered out of my mouth. "Really? You weren't *sure*? You know your father, Bay. The man had you tortured and thrown in a cell for lying to him, and that's just his most recent crime."

He winced, distress in his eyes. "I didn't know. I only did what I thought was best for us."

My chest hurt. Something stung in my heart. The scene before me twisted, and I was Wendy, staring at Hook. He smelled mostly of ash, but beneath that was a far worse scent: the tang of blood. "You did what was best for yourself," I whispered. "If you had done what was best for us, once we were safe, days ago, you wouldn't have hidden the truth. You knew lying to us was wrong."

"I knew you'd want to go back." He swiped his hair away from his eyes again. "We couldn't afford to go back. We couldn't afford to be captured. The second my father came back, he would have killed you, Wind Song! You're most useful to them dead. I did what was best to save you."

Because he didn't believe I could save myself? My heart cracked; I swallowed the bitterness and didn't let any welling tears fall. "I thought you were better than him." The image of him sacrificing himself in the temple came to mind, but beside it, the thought of Tiger Lily already out of reach burned. So what if he was willing to sacrifice himself for his goals? It was clear he was also willing to sacrifice others. "You're exactly like your father. If you had just..." *Told me the truth, ages ago, all of it. But again and again, he hadn't.* I was foolish. Belief and trust and faith and dust could be magic, but it didn't just magically change people. Each person had to choose to do that themselves.

I turned my back on him. "Come on, Whisper. Let's go home. We'll find Tiger Lily, I promise."

The wounded look in her eyes didn't hurt half as much as the doubt. She had only just begun to believe in me, and now, thanks to Bay, all I could see on her face was pain and question.

Taking a shaky breath, I lifted my pinky. "I promise."

She glanced at Bay then at my hand. Biting her lip, she nodded, linking her finger with mine.

I clung to the action whether she felt it in her heart or not. Without looking back, I asked, "Skye, did you know the truth?"

A moment passed, and I already knew the answer. *Of course*. He knew Hook as well as his son, they shared everything, and the damn creature was exactly as he'd said: loyal. "I'm sorry," he replied, voice meek.

"I guess this is where we part ways." I blinked, and tears traced down my cheeks, but I refused to acknowledge the dampness.

Whisper's lips parted. "How will I..." She stopped, realizing. Already, even with dust, how could she possibly trust it enough to get home?

"Wind Song, please," Bay started, touching me.

A rush of air slammed into his chest, throwing him back. He crashed into a tree and winced, sliding down the bark to land on his ass in the foliage, but I had seen the moment his feet left the ground. If I could do that, I could get Whisper safely home.

"Good eve, Star Boy," I murmured. Supporting Whisper around the waist, I exhaled, peering through the canopy at the sky. Star-speckled as it was, I pinpointed home. My feet left the ground right as Bay gathered his bearings.

"Please!" He shouted over the wind building around us. "I went about it wrong, but I didn't mean— If I had known—"

Whatever else he said was lost in the gusts.

Exhaustion ached in my limbs by the time I landed with Whisper in Skyla. She released a held breath, but that was all. We both looked around. No signs of a war had touched Aire. Everything, for the most part, was quiet. Normal.

"They haven't come yet?" I took a step, but my head spun.

"Lyly!" Whisper caught me before my face landed in the dirt. "Are you okay?"

"I'm not used to my power, I guess." Or my trust had shaken. I had been so wrong. How was I supposed to keep things from falling apart when they already had?

"Flying is one thing, but flying and using the wind to carry someone..." I tried to shake off the nausea, but it didn't want to go anywhere.

Whisper scanned the empty market streets. Each stall had a brightly colored cloth hanging over the entry. Any scents of baked goods or warm food had long since dispersed, and now only dust swirled down the paths. "Since it doesn't seem like the pirates are here yet, let's get back to my house so you can rest for a bit."

I leaned on her, taking slow breaths and not bothering to soften my words. "Your house isn't here anymore." Neither of us had a home to go back to right now.

"Oh. Right." Her lips pressed tight, and I closed my eyes to avoid seeing the sorrow in her gaze. She gasped. "Moth prince! Adam lives by himself in the woods where the moths and silkworms breed. It's closer anyway, just past the goat stables."

No wonder she hadn't seemed worried about him. The island that housed a majority of the animals was at the opposite end of the disaster. "Will he be okay with us appearing in the middle of the night?"

"He's an introverted young man. I doubt he'll mind two pretty damsels on his doorstep, one of whom is very, very into him. If he does, I think he'll get over it." She began dragging me in that direction, murmuring, "Besides, what choice do we have? Hook's on his way, and you can barely walk."

I shuffled along with her as best I could. Crossing the swaying bridge, we found ourselves bombarded with the soft bleats of goats and sheep. A single shepherd lay snoozing at the pen exit, his staff laid against his side. Other than him, the few homes tucked among the fairy oaks were dark and hushed, void of life.

We continued through the spattered woods gleaming with silver dust until they thickened, and a simple cottage covered with vines and huge white flowers appeared. Whisper breathed a little sigh. Obscured by the trees as this place was—and not in the habit of stalking poor, innocent, young boys—I'd never seen where our prestigious Silk Moth Babysitter lived. It looked plucked straight from a fairytale. Huge moths with forest green wings the size of my hand dallied from one flower to the next to rest and seek mates.

"Isn't this enchanting?" she whispered like she was sharing a secret and didn't want Adam to hear. "I'm going to live here one day."

"It fits you perfectly," I whispered back, and she smiled. Airwoman, it was good to see her smile even if nerves still wound tight in her limbs.

She knocked on the door and waited, fidgeting slightly. A look of sheer terror overcame her, and her hand rushed to her tangled, unwashed hair, but it was too late. The door eased open a crack before swinging the full way.

"Whisper!" Adam's wide blue eyes clung directly to her, ignoring me like I didn't exist. "You…you're okay?" He swallowed and shook his head, scrubbing a hand over his short, dark hair. "I've gotta be dreaming. I saw…I saw your name on the list of people we lost in the attack."

She blushed, holding her gaze on the ground. "It's a long story."

He looked at his bare chest and turned an impossible

shade of red that stood out even on his brown skin. "I—I'm so sorry. I wasn't expecting—" He glanced at me as though seeing me for the first time.

I lifted my hand in a pitiful greeting.

His brows lowered, and he looked past us, scanning the bloom-invested area. "Is everything okay?"

Whisper's smile wobbled. "Not really. Can we come in?"

He nodded without hesitation and stepped aside. Whisper helped me into the modest living room strewn with crocheted blankets and embroidered pillows. I landed on top of a pillow boasting the same kind of moth that lingered outside and reclined gratefully into the couch.

Adam sat across from us in a loveseat, moving aside a most recent embroidery project that made my brows furrow. He wasn't what I'd call a small guy or the type to live in this pastel-washed place.

"You live here alone?" I blurted.

Whisper jabbed me with her elbow. He laughed, smiling kindly. "It's okay. Yes, I do. My friends like to call my home, 'Grandma's Cottage.'"

I swept my eyes over the room again, rested on Whisper's tiny frown, and mumbled, "Really? That's odd. No idea why."

She shook her head and sighed, pushing my comments aside. "We need a favor. The pirates that attacked us several weeks ago aren't finished."

Adam's smile dropped away, and he cupped a hand against his mouth, leaning forward, pensive. "I know. There have been more sightings. As we've worked to rebuild, we've also been preparing for the worst. We know they have magic. Any time Peter and the Lost Boys get close to one, they use a spell and vanish."

Whisper's wide eyes turned on me. "What are they doing? You don't think..."

"Probably." I nodded. "They don't play fair. They are going to get all the information they can about where they'll be fighting and what they'll be up against." Thing was, Skyla didn't have a formal military or army or fighting force. We merely had our location that kept us separate from the world and a handful of children who practiced with wooden swords as it crossed their fancy. Something told me that this time, a group of pre-teens wasn't going to cut it.

The same thoughts rolled through Whisper's eyes like a storm, and she looked at Adam, biting her lip. "My mother comes from a magical place called Neverland. That's where she took me when our home fell. That's where Lyric and I have been. Now, she's been captured by Hook, and we know he plans to attack."

"Hook?" Adam breathed, straightening in his chair. "But that... He's always been just another one of Peter's fairytales, the villain behind his trophy pirate ship."

"The pirate ship is Peter's trophy for defeating Hook." I swallowed rising bile. "But I guess he didn't defeat Hook quite as well as he thought."

Adam's calm never broke, but he mussed his short hair and breathed deeply, pinning Whisper with his gaze. "You said you needed a favor? How can I help? Anything you need, anything at all..."

Her cheeks darkened as her eyes ran over him. "Just a place to stay for tonight. Lyric's exhausted, which is something of another story. In simple terms, she's our only hope of defeating Hook again, and then she's a piece of a much larger picture. Our world is in trouble."

"I apparently have eleven siblings that our goddess mother abandoned in each kingdom to protect from villains just like Hook. As we come into our magic, it no longer is a barrier over our homes." I didn't let the shock on Adam's face faze me. "I'm supposed to find them and save the world after I destroy a magical relic and after I save Skyla."

His mouth opened and closed twice before he managed, "Sounds…simple enough." He shook his head, moving forward in the conversation. "Of course you both can stay here. I'm sorry I don't have much space, but you're welcome to the couch, and then Whisper can have my bed in the back room." He glanced at her, linking his fingers between his knees. "If you'd like?"

Whisper murmured, "Where are you going to sleep?"

He chuckled. "If I can sleep after this information, right here. I expect, instead, to finish that, though." Gesturing at the half-complete embroidery circle, he shrugged. His smile softened, and there was love in it as he traced patterns on the rug with his toe. "I'm really glad you're okay, Whisper. I didn't know what to think when I saw your name with the…missing. After what happened at your birthday party, I thought that would be enough excitement for a while." His clasped hands tightened, and his lips pursed, emotion clogged in his throat as he repeated, "I'm just really glad you're okay."

Whisper sat still beside me, watching him as her eyes glassed. Sighing, I jabbed her with my elbow and motioned with my eyes for her to get her pretty little ass over there. She looked at me like I had grown two heads.

Adam cleared his throat, and the moment was gone. "I don't mind you both staying here, of course, but why didn't you go to Peter? Is the secret of his home that strict?"

My heart sank. "Not really. Not right now, anyway. Just..." My voice faded, and I took a breath. "Well, you know Peter. Everyone knows Peter. I've been gone for a while. I don't think he—" My throat closed, and I closed my eyes to avoid unleashing tears. Today had been hard enough without dwelling on this.

Whisper slipped her hand around mine and squeezed the same moment Adam said, "Oh. Right. His memory." He took a breath, then added, "I'm so sorry," like he was wishing me his condolences. Adam stood, delicately setting the matter aside. "If either of you would like something to eat, or a shower, or just anything, you're welcome to it. I can make tea?"

I'd seen why Whisper liked him before, but he was absolutely a prince, an angel. An angel with a four-pack. Airwoman, there was nothing bad to say about him. Except that he made me think about my demon.

Whisper kissed my hand before releasing it and standing to meet him in the middle of the room. "A shower and tea sound incredible."

Every muscle in his body relaxed, and he brushed her tangled, curly hair away from her forehead before bending to peck it. He whispered something to her that I couldn't make out, but whatever secret it was, she turned a deeper shade of cherry red.

Without missing a beat, Adam met my eyes. "Tea?"

I wordlessly nodded and hoped that it, plus a night of rest, would prepare me for tomorrow. Whatever Bay had done, Wendy didn't deserve her fate. I still had the vial that held the precise amount to heal her, and I still needed to find the Fountain so I could destroy it. If possible, before Hook had any chance of finding it as well.

28TH NOVEMBER

"Lyric!"

I gasped awake, staring blearily up at a face too close to mine to make out. I slashed my arm out, grabbing the air around me like a cloak and throwing it over the person. They moved effortlessly out of the way, but something broke across the room.

Scrambling for purchase, I blinked against the darkness, glanced at the chair where Adam had been when I drifted off, then swallowed when I found him missing.

The shadowy form hovering in the room was too small to be Bay.

"Shout in her face again. That worked so well the first time," a high-pitched voice I didn't recognize snipped. A pixie zipped to me, tilting her head. "It's just us," she said gently.

"Tinkerbell?" I blurted, squinting at the boy behind her. *Peter*. Was I dreaming?

Tinkerbell buzzed right back to him and sat on the rim of his hat. "I think she's okay."

"Where have you been?" Peter demanded, throwing his arms out. "Do you know how hectic it has been around here since you left?"

I stared at him, mute. It made no sense for him to be here. How would he have known I was here?

"Well?" he prompted, his voice pitching higher.

"Neverland," I replied in disbelief. If this were real, Adam would be seated in his chair like he was when I'd fallen asleep, and Whisper would have heard us by now.

Almost on cue, the door to the back room creaked, and light flooded the space. I squinted through it as Peter whirled on Adam and Whisper.

Adam stood protectively before her, holding an oil lamp, but there was a significant amount of murder in her tired gaze as well. At least, until she saw Peter.

"What are you doing here?" Her eyes went wide.

Peter folded his arms. "Doesn't matter. What are you doing here?" He dismissed them both and directed that question at me, frowning. "There are pirates *everywhere*, and I haven't been able to find you for weeks. Why didn't you come home?"

I swallowed, my heart rate picking up. "I," I began, my eyes filling with tears, "I didn't think you'd remember me."

His arms loosened, and his shoulders drooped for half a second. Hurt flickered through his gaze, but he shook it off. "Stupid."

"It's a valid point," Tinkerbell chimed mercilessly, kicking her legs through his hair.

Peter ignored her. "Well, I do remember you, so come home. We're on the edge of a war, and it's not just here either. This whole world is falling apart."

"I know that. I'm supposed to fix it." Though *how exactly* was another topic.

"Fix it?" He blinked at me, incredulous. "I don't think so. You're going to stay safe and let me handle this. It isn't the first time I've had to deal with pirates."

After everything, he thought I was just going to sit by and let him fight this battle alone? I rose off the couch, folding my arms as I faced him in the air. "It isn't exactly my first time dealing with them now, either."

"Lyric," he warned.

"No. I don't want to hear it. You've kept me on these islands for my entire life. And, sure, maybe when I left, I wasn't in the best mindset, but even then, I survived. And not only did I survive, I survived a place that's more dangerous than anywhere I've ever heard of. I came out of it all stronger." My fists clenched. "Skyla is my home. I'm going to stand beside you and defend it."

"This isn't an adventure!" he yelled. "This is war! And I'm—" His voice cracked. "I'm not going to lose you to it."

"For the love of the stars," Tinkerbell sighed dramatically, "Peter, she's two feet off the ground without pixie dust. I think she's learned a lot on her adventure. We've always known this day was coming. Or at least I have. Did you forget?"

He glared upwards, but didn't reply to her.

"What does she mean you've always known this day was coming?"

The annoyance on their faces disappeared. Peter's arms dropped by his sides, and his eyes went huge.

Whisper coughed, sidling up to me and wrapping her arms around my shoulders. "Yeah, she also understands pixies now. So maybe it's time to stop treating her like a child?"

Tinkerbell's breath seemed to hold, then she murmured, "So you really have been to Neverland, and it decided to grant you our tongue."

"I have. And we know that Hook is coming to try and take Skyla. And we know that he's not alone; he has magic, an enchantress backing him up."

Whisper nodded. "And also, he has my mother hostage."

Peter's concern was blank, but Tinkerbell's eyes shone with something deeper, and she whispered, "Hook is back, and he has Tiger Lily?"

Sunlight gleamed through the window, catching on Adam standing patiently in the hall. Dawn meant we hopefully had another day before Hook could reach us. I landed with my feet on the floor and found my bag where I'd discarded it beside the couch the night before. It had definitely seen better days, but it would still carry food for the trip to the Fountain. Other than that, my spyglass and pan flute were all that had survived Neverland. I hesitated before picking it up. "We have to find and destroy the Fountain of Youth before Hook even has a chance to reach it. He wants to use the magic for himself and in whatever plot the enchantress has set him on."

Tinkerbell flitted off Peter's hat and waved her hands before my bag, blocking me from grabbing it. "You know about the Fountain?"

"Yes. Do you know where it is?"

Her gaze dropped, and she landed on the flap of my satchel. "I vaguely remember."

"Home, right?"

She straightened, holding herself in a hug. Her huge eyes met mine, and she swallowed, nodding.

"No way." Whisper threw her hair back and blew out a breath. "All this time, the Fountain has been in your home?"

"Hidden under it." I snatched my bag strap, and Tinkerbell moved out of the way so I could pull it around my shoulders. My eyes caught on the feathers marking my arm, and I clenched my jaw. Exhaustion punctuated my movements, but I would have to accept the fact I hadn't had much sleep. "Right under my nose, just like the temple spirit said."

"Forgotten in time by the only one who had ever been allowed to find it." Tinkerbell exhaled, looking at Peter. "It was ages ago, back when Skyla had first appeared in this world as a refuge for those fleeing Neverland's tyrants."

"How do the other Lost Boys share his eternity if only he found it so long ago?"

Sadness made Tinkerbell settle back into the dip of Peter's hat, her legs pulled tight against her chest. "After the first war with Hook, Peter took a blood oath, promising to protect the Lost Boys who survived; unknowingly, he bound them to the power running through his veins."

Peter scratched his head, peering at us all like we were talking in another language. At least, he understood both of us, though. Whisper tugged on my sleeve, a brow quirked in question.

"They shared blood," I said.

"Oath blood," Peter added, and something lit in his

eyes, but it was gone in the next second. He pumped his chest. "None of whatever you're talking about matters. If pirates are on their way, we need to secure Skyla. And that means getting you home."

I frowned. "How did you even know I was here?"

His expression didn't change as he tried to push me toward the door. "Doesn't matter."

"You don't remember, do you?" Whisper accused.

Peter glared at her, but that was exactly it.

I looked directly at Tinkerbell, even though she had sunk deep into the groove of Peter's hat, hiding everything but her leaf-clad feet from view. "Someone told us. The other boy who also glitters with pixie dust."

Bay.

He had followed us? He was here?

My heart wouldn't settle from the moment it knew Bay had followed us back to Skyla. I floated in a daze toward home, ignoring all Peter's complaints about "strangers discovering the base" even as he led us there. Whisper ignored him too, guiding me along behind her like a balloon. Periodically, she shot me a worried glance, but I tried to smile and reassure her when I noticed.

He was here, in the shadows. He knew where our home was. Had telling Peter where I was been to distract him? Had Bay figured out where the Fountain was, even though I'd never said anything specific about its location?

Worry ate away at my gut, and I tried to temper it. Bay was still Bay. Even if what he'd done concerning Tiger Lily was unforgivable, he wasn't the kind of person who would...go behind our backs and burn down an entire civilization of people, right? I had seen in his second temple test that he had boundaries.

I squeezed Whisper's hand and hoped. He had proven himself to be like his father in too many ways. My heart still wanted to believe in him, but I couldn't afford misplaced trust in these dire moments before what could be the devastation of the entire world.

Peter grumbled the entire way down the tunnel into the base, swiping the furs aside. Whisper followed. I followed behind her, spotting the Lost Boys at the table, their hands filled with food. They peered at one another, then back at Whisper, but no recognition touched their gazes.

"Ah..." Slightly began, "Who're these girls, Peter?"

A part of me chipped away. Peter had remembered, but they hadn't? I looked between the Twins, but they shifted their gaze to one another, exchanging shrugs. Tootles' brows were lowered with concentration, but nothing sparked, and for some reason, that made him deflate in sorrow. One by one, each turned away to wait for Peter's answer.

"What do you mean? It's Lyric," Peter snapped, finding his chair and plopping into it.

"Lyric?" Nibs scrubbed the edge of an empty bowl against his head. "Is that a new friend of yours?"

Peter sighed, waving a hand at them, and a sliver of brokenness splintered over his face. He wiped it away when he looked at Whisper and I. "Your room is untouched, and there should be enough food in the stores."

Swallowing the lump burning in my throat, I nodded and crossed to the door.

"Her room?" Chubs and some others chorused behind me.

"I always wondered why we had that."

Someone said with a scrunched nose, "So girly."

My stomach tightened, but I pushed into my space and let the familiar glowing mirabel, bed, and random bits and bobs calm me. They did a poor job.

"It's just like I would have imagined!" Whisper laughed, though the sound was strained. She lifted a hand-made arrow off a dresser and twirled the shaft between her fingers. "I can't believe it took this long for me to finally see your home."

I couldn't believe it took me this long to really see how fractured my family was. What did the world look like through their eyes, when everything was new and remade and the games they played again and again were always the same but never recalled? I didn't know how often the Fountain's magic reset them, but it was clear only Peter knew how to tamper with it.

And he fought. He fought to keep me.

A sob swallowed me up, and I gasped, leaning against the dirt wall and covering my face with my hands.

Whisper set the arrow down and was at my side in an instant. "Hey," she said softly, "it's okay. Let it out."

Tears poured down my cheeks, and strangled breaths left my chest. I hadn't cried like this since that night I thought I'd lost her. Now, she held me, letting me muffle my pain against Adam's shirt, the one he gave her after she showered with his soap; she smelled like a stranger, and that made my sobs worse.

I stayed in her arms for several long minutes. Eventually, the tears dried, but the ache in my chest remained. "Let's find that accursed Fountain and get rid of it," I whispered. I took a few spare moments to change out of the clothes I had borrowed from a native camp in Neverland. Promising to avenge them once and for all, I pulled on my own familiar shirt and pants.

Whisper scratched her moccasin against the corner of my rug. "You said the Fountain was under your home. How do we get under this?" She looked at the hard dirt floor, and her nose pinched. "Do we just dig?"

A flutter zipped into the room, and Tinkerbell swept her gaze over me before tilting her head. Some emotion filled her eyes, but neither her voice nor her countenance conveyed it. "I can lead you to the entrance. The Fountain itself is under our home, but you can't reach it by digging." She flew within an inch of my face and narrowed her eyes. "But before I take you to one of the most powerful relics in the world, how do you plan to destroy it exactly?"

I scrubbed my cheek, taking deep breaths, then muttered, "I don't know. The spirit of the temple—"

"The temple?" she chimed.

"In Neverland."

Her eyes widened, and she jerked back. "You've spoken to the spirit of Neverland? You survived those tests?"

Dumbly, I nodded.

"What did she say?" Her words came airy and breathless, reverent, and her hands clasped in prayer.

"'All wind that rises must fall.' I don't know what it means. I just assume it has something to do with my powers." I wiped my hands on my shirt and offered Whisper a weak smile. It was all I could manage. "Tink's going to take us to the Fountain."

Tinkerbell shook her head. "No, no. I'm going to lead you to the entrance, but I'm not going there again. That magic is a drug. If Neverland trusts you to handle it, then I will too, but I can't go back. I just can't."

"What did she say?" Whisper asked.

"She's leading us to the start, but we have to make it from there on our own." Biting my lip, I clenched a fist around my bag strap.

Tinkerbell raised her head, eyeing Whisper haughtily. "Does your friend have what it takes to make it out of there, Lyric? If Neverland entrusted you with this, I'm sure you'll be fine, but..."

"Whisper made it through the temple's tests, as well." I frowned.

Tinkerbell zipped to my ear, brushing my hair aside and whispering like someone else in the room could understand her. "But, she can't even fly."

I swatted at her. "Yes, she can."

"Oh, really?" Tinkerbell's brows shot up, but her expression remained indignant. She fluttered over Whisper, then pulled back and crossed her arms as pixie dust rained into my friend's light curls.

Whisper looked at me, shaking her head. "Oh, no. No, I don't think— Not after..."

"You said it before, even if I didn't realize it then. You weren't flying because you trusted Skye." I held out my hand. "You never trusted them, and you were right. I should have listened closer to what you were telling yourself in the temple, but why could you fly?"

She looked at my hand, her brows knitted. I floated off the ground, and realization overcame her. "I trusted you wouldn't let me fall." Clasping my hand, she grinned, throwing a sassy look at Tinkerbell before curtseying into the air. "Guess both our heads were a little jumbled after all that, but yes, little miss priss, I can fly."

"Hmm," Tinkerbell tittered, "interesting. I've never seen someone regain their ability to fly."

"Maybe she never lost it. Maybe she just needed to remember that she wasn't afraid of falling because there was still someone who wouldn't let her, no matter what."

Tinkerbell shrugged. "Well, nothing regarding Neverland is straightforward or makes sense, and we—the pixies—were birthed there, so naturally, our magic reacts in questionable ways. One thing is clear, you both were accepted. And if Mother accepts you, so will I." Her eyes darted, and she huffed. "Come, I'm sure we don't have much time."

I landed as soon as Tinkerbell zipped out of the room. Whisper landed beside me, skeptical. "You're still not feeling well, are you?"

"Barely any sleep after flying us both between entire worlds? No wonder I'm not in my best shape." I sighed, squeezing her hand. "We'll get through this. After all," I straightened, fluttering my lashes, "we have been treated to mythical moth prince tea. Don't you dare think I didn't notice you both coming out of the bedroom an hour ago."

She flushed. "There was a lot on your mind. Of course, you didn't notice."

"His hair was all ruffled, and I'm certain the dark promise in your gaze was a reaction to interruption, not threat."

She snatched her hand out of mine to press against her breast. "My my, Lyly. How soon we forget. It was you who told me to tempt him. But don't we have more important things to dwell on, aside from my dreams coming true in the moments before the world could very well cease to exist as we know it?"

"Yes,"—Tinkerbell zipped back into the room, her hands on her hips—"we do. Now hurry up!"

Whisper glanced at me, then at Tinkerbell's trail as she left once more. "I almost understood that one." She chuckled, touching my shoulder. "Are you okay?"

I peered at the mostly closed door, hearing the Lost Boys murmuring beyond it, and took a deep breath before nodding. "I'm trying to be. Peter remembers. Relationships can be rebuilt. We just have to make sure there's a place to rebuild."

"Let's do just that."

I thought I'd explored every nook and cranny on two Skyla islands: the mainland and home. Turns out, I had missed a hidden cavern nestled a ways past Peter's tree. Beyond the pond where we always played while I was growing up, within the cleft of a sheer rock wall covered in brambles, there lay a single section of vines that clung to nothing but air. The opening was little more than two feet across at its base, and we would have to crawl through there since it only narrowed into a crack at the top.

"Be careful," Tinkerbell said, giving my cheek a quick hug. "The closer you get to the magic, the stronger its allure. You'll find reasons you need it, but nothing is worth that power." Her eyes flicked to Whisper, and she pressed her lips together. "Be each other's strength."

"How did you overcome it?" I asked.

She puffed her chest and folded her arms like I had insulted her. "I have no use for such a thing when I'm beside Peter. A pixie's life is extended through belief. As long as he believes in me, I will remain. And I will protect. And I will love." Her cheeks tinted crimson, but she nodded before saying more, and she was gone.

Whisper nudged aside the brambles and looked at the small space we'd have to squeeze through with pursed lips before judging her midsection and bosom with an exaggerated sigh. "Any final wisdom from her ladyship?"

"We have to be one another's strength to make it through this." I crouched, squinting into the dark. It lightened toward the end of what I could see, the same flowers that grew on my ceiling blooming along the walls. "Also, I think she's in love with Peter, which is just weird on a million levels. I'm sharing so I don't have to suffer that knowledge alone."

Whisper's nose scrunched. "Okay, I'm more than happy to face certain doom to get that picture out of my mind. Are you ready?"

"As I'll ever be."

Together, we slipped into the coolness of the cave. A tingle ran down my spine, and the hair on my arms raised the second I was immersed in the space. Whisper met my gaze, took a deep breath, and tugged Adam's shirt sleeves over her hands.

We moved on. I waited for something to take over, for some sense of magic to overwhelm me and steal my thoughts away, but minutes passed, drifting into an hour, and only the flowered walls met my view. The tunnel wound like a snake, twisting and coiling, sometimes inclining and sometimes declining.

"Are we actually getting any closer?" Whisper asked after any initial fear or resolution had worn off.

"I can't tell," I replied, exhaling. I checked the air to see where we stood and what we might be looking forward to. There were only two streams of wind flow, a massive, rushing one before us, and a quiet, seeping one behind us. But there were two touches of something more back there too, something irregular.

I froze.

"What is it?" Whisper asked.

I swallowed, gripping my bag until my knuckles went white. "He's here." He'd followed us. But, of course, he had. We already knew he'd come with us to Skyla, and finding the Fountain had been his sole purpose all along. My empty sheath weighed more on my thigh than it did when it was full, and my fingers found it with a level of dread. Even if I had my knife, could I fight Bay with it?

Perhaps the real question was: would he fight me with the knives I knew he had?

The thought broke my heart.

When the path jackknifed, creating a bend where we wouldn't be seen, Whisper and I stopped, waiting. Sure enough, after several minutes, Bay drifted around the corner silently, spotted us, and went still. Our eyes locked, and my chest pinched. Before I could say anything, he raised his hands and blurted, "You can't destroy the Fountain until I save my mother. That's the only reason I'm here."

Whisper snarled, "Oh, so now you're interested in saving mothers, huh?"

True remorse seemed to flicker through his gaze when he looked at her, but he shook his head and pinned his eyes back on me. "Please. Try to believe me. This is all I've lived for since I lost her. It's only Skye and I. Any friends I had are more than twice my age now or no longer have any qualms about beating me to a pulp."

I wanted to believe him. Believing in the people I cared about came so easily to me, but he'd abandoned Tiger Lily and didn't tell us. Worse, he led us to believe she was okay, knowing his own lie.

Whisper gripped my hand. "We don't believe liars."

"Wind Song," he begged, disregarding her completely.

I dropped my gaze. "We are going to save your mother, Bay. I still have the vial, and I will make sure the water gets to her."

"But—"

"No buts," I snapped, glaring. Releasing Whisper's hand, I took a deep breath and raised my head. "We can collect water just as well as you can. Unlike some of us, we aren't in the habit of ignoring people our friends care about."

"Maybe try trusting in us for a change." Whisper

tossed back her hair and huffed. "If it bites you in the rear, you deserved it."

Skye clenched his fists and fluttered before Bay. "These walls are lined with the same magic that courses through the temples in Neverland."

"He's right. The further you go, the stronger the magic gets. It's safer toge—" Bay pleaded, hands outstretched.

"Thank you." Whisper scoffed. "We already know that."

"Tinkerbell told us what to expect." I held his gaze, though the desperation in it burned in my gut. "We have each other; we know we can count on each other."

He deflated, hearing what I hadn't said. He'd proven that we couldn't count on him. He couldn't be trusted.

"I'll know if you follow us," I said. "So don't."

Lamely, he nodded, looked at the cave wall, and floated to it, sliding to the ground. "I'll be here then." He drew his legs up and clasped his hands between his knees, no longer daring to glance at us. "Good luck."

Before I was sure I had done the right thing, Whisper grabbed my arm and pulled me along with her. When I peered over my shoulder, Bay's head was in his hands, and his whole body shook with tears.

It didn't take long after we left Bay to come upon the Fountain. It was unlike anything I'd ever seen, and neither of the temple visions had done it justice. The mirabel clinging to the cracks in the ceiling tripled in mass, boasting luminous blooms twice the size of my head. The blossoms flooded the space with light, revealing a pit that led into churning waves.

That pit stood between us and the Fountain. It sprayed gold, glittering water over the edges of several wide bowls. Intricate designs depicting a history I hardly knew decorated the pearl dishes. Just the sight of it all left me breathless.

Whisper touched my shoulder, her eyes pinned on the magnificent structure. "Can you believe it? All this time, right beneath our feet." Her voice drifted off, and I checked to make sure she was still with me. Nothing glassed her eyes when I met them, and I exhaled with relief.

A distinct tang of magic vibrated in the wind, skating down my throat when I parted my lips. "It's beautiful."

Moments passed, each of us staring and waiting.

"Do you feel any different?" Whisper asked finally.

My head shook. "No, you? Any urge to join the forever-twelve cult?"

"Pardon you. I'd be forever nineteen. And I think I'll pass." Holding my wrist, she leaned to look into the swirling ocean. "The only way across is over. How are you feeling?"

An ache spread through my chest before dipping into my stomach. "Still incapable. I'm not sure I'm willing to take the risk. If I drop you…" Bitterness overwhelmed the taste of magic on the back of my tongue. "I'm not willing to take that chance."

Her brows furrowed. "What are you saying?"

I sifted through my bag, drawing out the vial and

clasping it in my hand. "The faster I get over there and back here, the better. It should only take a moment."

"And if something goes wrong?" Lips pursed, she narrowed her eyes. "You're also supposed to destroy that, remember? How are you going to manage *that* quickly?"

Sensing skepticism, I smiled. "I can see you're getting defensive, but trust me. I've lived with the forever-twelve cult. There is no way I'm joining it at any age." I lifted off the ground, but she didn't release my wrist.

"Be careful. If something starts to go wrong, you come right back, and we'll figure things out from there."

I nodded. Dread showered me, cold and murky, but I didn't let it show. She let me go, and I faced the magical pool of golden ichor. Crossing over the pit of waves and secrets, I felt a hot pour of the spirit's words come to the forefront of my mind.

All wind that rises must fall.

Was I supposed to somehow push the Fountain into that pit, into the ocean?

I landed on the other side, and sweat coated my skin. Doubts bombarded me. If I couldn't even fly Whisper here, how was I supposed to—

"Are you still okay?" Whisper yelled.

My mouth was dry; my palms were clammy. "I'm fine!" I called back, not looking at her. "I think I need to get this thing in that thing."

"In the hole?" Surprise coated her tone, but when she spoke again, it had mellowed. "That makes sense. Do you think you can use your wind to get it there?"

No. "I'll try."

First things first, I tried to shake off the overpowering sensations burrowing into my skin. With every step closer, it seemed impossible. It was so strong. And I wasn't. No wonder Peter could do so many insane things. And I couldn't. He had drunk this stuff. And I hadn't.

My hand shook as I uncorked the vial and hovered the glass above the pool of water. A gentle mist fell before my eyes, the closer my fingers got to the liquid. To fill the vial, I would need to touch it. Touch the magic that had enough strength to provide people eternal life.

"Still okay?" Whisper's words were nearly lost beneath the sound of water.

I swallowed. I wasn't. I wasn't okay at all. So what if I believed in myself a little more now than I did before my adventure in Neverland? I still had to face a pirate that not even Peter had been able to get rid of.

I wasn't strong enough.

"Lyric?" Whisper's voice pitched.

I closed my eyes and filled the vial. Magic touched my fingers, permeated my flesh. It flooded my veins. If I wasn't strong enough, this would be. It had to be. Too much relied on me when I couldn't even rely on myself.

"Lyric!" Whisper yelled. "Lyric! No!"

Her scream filled my head the second I brought the vial to my lips. My fingers trembled, and I blinked, but it wasn't enough to draw me out of the haze. *I needed this.* If I didn't have this power, then I wouldn't be able to save Whisper, or Peter, or anyone on Skyla. This wasn't just a battle for Skyla, either. After this, should I succeed against Hook, I had to help save the world.

Squeezing my eyes shut, I—

"Nope." The firm word was said directly into my ear. A strong chest hit my back, and someone's hands gripped mine, stopping me from throwing the water down my throat. The person wrestled the cork out of my grasp and secured the vial before meeting my gaze. Hazel eyes.

Bay. *He wasn't supposed to be here.* They had warned me to make sure he didn't drink from the Fountain. It… didn't look like he was drinking? Brows drawn, he stared at me. My vision blurred, but I felt his lips against my cheek, and his exhale shook. "Let's get you out of here."

Everything went dark.

29TH NOVEMBER

Comfortable heat. Security. The gentle scent of ocean brine and magic. I breathed it in, drifting softly back into my dreams. Someone jostled my body, and that jerked me fully awake. My eyes snapped open, and hair brushed my cheek.

"Careful!" Whisper snapped. "You're going to drop her."

Bay hitched me up again. "Well, I don't see you offering to carry her."

"Give her here." Whisper shot him a tight-lipped smile and opened her arms.

"I knew we shouldn't have slept back there. First rule of life: don't sleep in a magic-tainted cave." Bay shook his head, and his loose hair tickled my cheek. "It's made you delusional."

"What else were we supposed to do? We'd been walking all day; she had fainted." She folded her arms. "I'm well-rested. I can carry my friend now."

"You really can't," Skye muttered. "You're like half

her size, and while she's asleep, she isn't aware enough to even unknowingly make herself lighter."

"Excuse me? What did he say?" she demanded.

"You've already got your shoulders full with Skye." Bay sighed, adjusting his hold on my thighs again.

It was in that exact instant I realized he was holding me by my thighs and keeping my chest pressed against his shoulder blades. I floundered, flailing backwards.

"H-hey!" he stammered, grappling for purchase, but I tumbled out of his grasp, managing to perform a back-flip midair before finding the ground with my feet. Bay blinked at me, looking me over. "I guess you're awake now?"

"Lyly! You're okay!" Whisper pounced, wrapping her arms around me in a full swing that made Skye retreat off her shoulder.

Memories flooded back, and I swallowed bile, the sensations of fog in my mind not fully abated. Lifting a hand, I jabbed a finger at Bay. "You followed us! We told you not to, but you did! We asked you to trust us, but you didn't. You didn't trust me! Again!"

"*What?*" He balked, an injured expression melding with exasperation. "I heard Whispering Meadow scream and came to the rescue. I'm your knight in shining armor."

"You didn't trust us!" I swayed into Whisper, and she held me up, grunting under my weight.

He folded his arms, ignoring how tipsy I was. "I did. I sat still, and I waited, and I developed a nervous habit of bouncing my leg, and then I heard a scream and thought maybe it was code for, 'something is wrong; send help.'"

I blinked at him, and my arm lowered.

"If you're speechless, may I suggest 'Thank you'?" Skye frowned at me, his tiny arms folded as he landed on Bay's shoulder.

Bay shook his head and dragged his fingers through his hair. "Actually, I'd be happy if you consider it the beginning of an apology. I want to help make things right because you were right. I was selfish. Just like my father, I convinced myself I meant well, but I didn't want to risk forfeiting the Fountain or getting what I needed for my mother, even if it meant sacrificing yours…" He winced, moving his gaze to Whisper. "Not even. She isn't just your mother; she was my friend. And I threw that away."

Remorse touched his lips, plucking the strings of my heart. Swallowing, I murmured, "You didn't take any of the water?"

"Just the vial."

"Didn't you hear the temptations?" Even now, doubts floated in my ears, beckoning me to turn back. If Whisper weren't holding me upright, I didn't know if I'd obey them or not.

He shrugged, scuffing his hair a final time and dropping his arm. "Sure. But I was a bit too worried about you to listen to them. They promised useless things anyway." A secret hid beneath the pain in his smile, and I wanted to know what it was, but I couldn't find the words to ask.

"You two can talk after we confirm my mother is safe. Before then, you're still on probation, and I refuse to give Lyric my blessing. That is to say, I'm still not convinced you won't hurt her like your father hurt Wendy."

His fists clenched, and his gaze blackened, but he steadied his breaths and turned on his heel. "Fine. That's fair. If I can prove it to you, then maybe I'll be able to prove it to myself, too. And if I can prove it to myself, maybe I'll finally be free of his shadow."

I reached for him, clutching his shirt.

He jerked away before looking over his shoulder. His eyes widened, then softened. "How are you feeling?"

"Awake." And very, very reluctant to be.

"It's a start." His feet left the ground, and he focused on the path ahead. "We've been in here for a day and a half. Magic stretches the tunnel, making it difficult to get in or out, but we should be getting close. The flowers are thinning."

I squinted at the ceiling. He was right. I hadn't even noticed.

"Do you think you can walk?" Whisper asked.

"Maybe?" Leaning off her support, I found my balance, and my head settled some. "Yeah. I'm all right." I wiped my forehead, but it was dry. Why did I feel so hot? "I didn't drink any of that stuff, right?"

Whisper paled, looking at Bay.

He shook his head. "No, I made it in time."

A wash of ice hit me. "I never destroyed it. We have to go back. I'm supposed to destroy it."

"There is no way we're going back there." Whisper folded her arms and glared at me.

I turned, starting back. "But I promised."

Bay landed in front of me, arms folded. His mouth opened, but he never got a chance to speak. Reverberating thuds vibrated down the walls, hammering into my skull, and shaking the Fountain's grip free at last.

Clarity shot through my veins like adrenaline.

"The warning gong…" Whisper's hair rose on her arms. "That has to mean they're here. This is it."

"We don't have a second to waste." Bay nodded at Skye, and he doused Whisper in fresh dust before stopping in front of me. I was already off the ground. Panic, determination, and fear wound so tight in my stomach, I could hardly catch a breath. Bay grabbed my arm before I had the chance to move. "Here," he said, offering me one of his knives. "You're not going up there defenseless."

I looked at the gleaming metal. It shone blue in the flower light. Wind touched my skin, and I held onto it, curling it around all of us. I wasn't defenseless, but I wouldn't turn down a weapon. "Thank you." Taking it, I delivered the blade to my sheath. It didn't fit quite right, but that mattered little.

"This is it," I echoed. A hypnotic whisper touched my thoughts, calling me back to the Fountain, claiming I had to destroy it, but I didn't have time to dwell on the alluring voice. I would destroy it. But that would have to wait.

We crawled out of the cave into the blaring notes of the gong. Night surrounded us, and I paled, seeing that the purple hint of twilight still cradled the sky. We had been trapped in there far longer than we'd thought.

The pirates came under the guise of night. But, of course, they did. If they came from the sky using some sort of magic to fly, they had to. My heart pounded in my chest, and my breaths wouldn't settle. *This was it.* The battle. The one I had failed to prevent. Things had gotten so out of hand since I left for Neverland.

Mouth dry, I soared above the trees, Whisper and Bay at my sides. Ships. Not one. Not two. Dozens. Dozens of ships speckled the sky, glowing like stars with the magic that held them afloat. I shuffled through my bag and drew out my spyglass. Peering through it, I went deathly still.

Tiger Lily stood beside Hook at the helm of the largest sloop. His metal hand stroked her cheek.

"What do you see?" Whisper choked, clutching my sleeve.

"Tiger Lily is okay. She's alive, and she doesn't look hurt."

"Oh, thank the airwoman," she breathed, and some tension around Bay eased as well.

I looked at him, pinpointing Skye on his shoulder. "We'll need all hands on deck. Even the small ones."

He nodded stiffly. "I'm running on empty, and Bay's low on dust; don't let him fall. I'll be back."

Habitually, Bay began braiding his hair, freezing when he seemed to remember he didn't have anything to hold it back.

"What is it?" Whisper asked.

"I lost my tie somewhere a few days ago." His lips pursed. "I can't fight well if it's loose."

"Don't you have a backup?" Whisper sneered.

Bay scoffed. "I'm not a girl."

Rolling my eyes, I grounded myself in their banter. "Use a reed or vine."

"Or hack it off." Whisper folded her arms.

"Don't you dare." I scowled at him. "Use a reed or a vine, and please, both of you."—I took a shaking breath —"we need to be on the same team here." Lowering my spyglass, I bagged it and brushed the handle of the dagger Bay had given me. "This is war."

"We'll never make it against those numbers. We need to somehow get an advantage." Whisper's brow furrowed, stiffness in her form. Something lit in her eyes. "Our pirate ship. It still has ammo inside. If I can get the cannons to work, maybe we can at least take out some of the ships?"

"Perfect. Gather the people who aren't trained to fight and head there. Tiger Lily is front and center, so watch where you aim, and watch your dust or replenish." The idea of her being inside a pirate ship, safely away from the thick of the battle, settled my nerves, but the idea of her leaving me in this moment made my heart jump erratically. "Be careful."

"Look who's talking." She threw her arms around me and squeezed. "I will never abandon you."

"We will never be apart," I murmured.

With those words, she zipped away, landing and running through the trees until I couldn't see her anymore.

Anxiety fought for a hold on me, but I couldn't let it take over. I believed in myself. If I didn't, I wouldn't be flying right now. "We need to meet up with Peter."

"Unless I'm mistaken, he's way ahead of you." Bay pointed at a streak of orange and green. I squinted, making out Peter hovering before the armada. He glowed, a different shade than the ships, but he was little more than a speck against the pale blue, ever-darkening sky; they were foreboding suns.

My heart jerked, and I was flying toward him before I could think, Bay hot on my heels.

"Wind Song!" he shouted, and I whirled in time to see him drop.

My stomach fled, and I shot after him, reaching for the wind to grasp his body and carry him safely to the ground. When he had landed, I hit the earth, panting. "Are you okay?" I stammered. "I'm so sorry. I didn't think you were that low on dust, and I was focused on—"

A cannon fired; my lungs tightened. Any words I was saying deserted my mind and my mouth.

"It's okay." Bay held my shoulders, and worry swam in his eyes, but he found half a smile to offer me. "I already fell for you once."

I stared at him, ignoring the flush running over my cheeks. *Everything could go wrong*. Another cannon fired. *I could lose it all.* Wincing, I linked my hand around the back of his neck and pulled his lips to mine. Tears pooled in my eyes as I kissed him quick. "Wait for Skye," I said, pulling away. "And don't do anything stupid."

I turned, but he caught my wrist. "Like running into battle alone?"

"I'm not alone. I never have been. Even when I thought my mother had abandoned me here, people surrounded me and gave me a home. My strength comes from each and every one of you. Each breath alone may not be much, but together, they create a storm." I held his gaze and hoped he didn't see the way terror consumed me.

Whether he did or not, his grip loosened. "I believe in you, Wind Song. But that doesn't mean I'm not scared of losing you."

I was scared of losing everything, and I didn't have time to waste. The second he released me, I left, pushing myself to meet Peter in the air.

Head raised, arms folded, cannons blasting behind us toward the ships, Peter barely glanced my way.

"How can you not remember me?" Hook sputtered, his face red with rage. He had dragged Tiger Lily to the front of the ship, and both of them were pressed tight against the deck rail.

Peter shrugged. "Maybe you just weren't entirely too memorable?"

Tinkerbell laughed, the chiming sounds too merry for the moment.

"You!" Hook spat, lifting his metal hand off Tiger Lily to jab toward me as though just noticing I had appeared. "You remember me, don't you?"

Peter looked at me then, raising a brow.

I caught the unspoken glimpse of mischief in his eye and tilted my head. The bundled nerves in my stomach settled, if a little. "Not sure? You have one of those faces. I think I've seen it before, maybe? But then again, maybe not."

Hook blustered, slashing his arm outwards, accidentally smashing his hook into Smee's face. The stout man collapsed, but his captain couldn't care less. "What madness are you spouting, girl? You were with my son just days ago!"

"Son?" Peter's brows lifted. He floated to my back, all

gloat and pride as he presented me. "Hey, that's neat! This is my daughter. Where's your kid?"

Hook snapped. My heart soared with strength and confidence.

"Attack!" Hook yelled.

I didn't need a command. Both Peter and I rose through the night sky, our arms bent at our waists. Our crow rang above the cannon fire, the shouts, the buzz of pixie wings. Everything in that moment was adrenaline, excitement, assurance. There's no way we could lose.

Out of nowhere, the Lost Boys swooped in, diving for Tiger Lily. Their whoops and wallops overlaid the pirates' yells. Cannons went off from Hook's ships, targeting Aire. I felt the wind breathe through me, swirl around me, and I sent the lead balls tumbling right back.

Hook screeched, jumping away from Tiger Lily as one ball crashed through the deck right next to him.

"You missed, Lyric!" Peter teased.

I smirked, brushing away the sweat beading on my forehead; moving lead wasn't exactly the easiest thing in the world, but I had done it. "I'd like to see you do better!"

He flourished a bow. "My pleasure." Drawing his knife, he waggled his brows and zoomed toward Hook.

"Bring her ashore!" Hook hollered, catching Peter out of the corner of his eye. He drew his sword the moment Peter landed on the cannonball protruding from the deck. The pirate crew circled the orange-haired boy, but Hook sneered. "This one's mine."

"Hmm." Peter twirled his blade. "Bold words for a codfish."

The pirate's eyes alighted, teeth baring in a foul grin beneath his waxed mustache. Blades sang in battle, and I turned my attention to Tiger Lily. The Lost Boys had her. She was safe. But the ships were landing quickly, and there were still at least half a dozen to worry about. Whisper had done well, sending so many to the hungry ocean, but I supposed it was my turn. Landing in the clearing just before a break in the trees led to the city, I formulated a plan.

Pixies rushed from the woods and every island all around us, screaming their battle cries.

Skyla's people shouted and raised crude weapons above their heads. As the pirates dismounted, Skyla met them with fury and force.

This was *our* home. Hook had already stolen Neverland from us, taken Tiger Lily's family and culture, but her people remained here. My people remained here. We remained. And we weren't leaving any time soon.

My fingers brushed Bay's dagger, and my heart wanted to find him in the chaos, but Hook's ship hit the ground, plowing through trees and brush to skid to a stop before me. Atop it, Peter and Hook were locked in an ageless battle that had seen itself play out through generations.

Inhaling, I lifted my arms, fingers splayed. *Wings*. I pictured great feathered wings behind me, gathering the forces of air to my side. The smooth breeze thickened, pooling into a rushing fall. I careened it toward the ship, smashing into the bow with all the force of a hurricane. The wood creaked and groaned. The sails filled. The sloop bounced.

Concentration beaded on my brow, and panting breaths filled me.

"Blast!" Hook yelled, parrying one of Peter's blows and refinding his footing. "You're free to kill," he snapped at his crew.

The men chuckled as they threw themselves overboard. Their boots thumped into the dirt, and I narrowed my gaze at them, but I didn't let up. One way or another, I was getting this ship off my homeland.

"Need a hand?" Bay passed me, flashing me a smile, and lifting his cutlass. When I brightened, he winked, then dashed at my attackers.

Skye zipped off his shoulder and landed on mine. "Whatever is making those things fly, it isn't pixie dust. We can break the spell of the ones still airborne. Can you handle whatever lands?"

I threw a blast of wind toward a pirate, closing in on Bay's back and flung him off the island. "I think I can." Sweat plastered my hair to my cheeks, but I wasn't going to back down.

"I know you can." He nodded and was gone, calling an army of pixies to him with a shrill whistle. They dashed for the few ships still in the sky, firing cannonballs at Skyla.

I forced all the power I could manage into the gusts filling Hook's sloop's sails, and the ship hopped. Unwilling to relinquish the moment it was off-ground, I poured everything I had into billowing it over the edge.

Pirates tumbled off in the moments before the spell shattered, and the sloop plummeted.

Hook and Peter made it to land, Peter bowing toward me but never losing his stance with the captain.

Exhaustion played behind my eyes, but I managed a weak smile amid the budding headache. My focus fell on Bay next. He parried blows from three men, falling back with every hit. Ruthless, they attacked without form, intent on slashing their foe to bits by brute strength alone.

I took his side, drawing my knife. "Hi."

"Hey." His gaze found me for half a second; it was all the time we could spare on each other, but the way his smile brightened stuck with me as I sloppily diverted blow after blow. My arms rattled, and the impacts didn't help my blooming headache. Thankfully, our skills in close combat seemed equal. Unfortunately, they had strength I didn't.

I tried to power my attacks with wind, but the gales deflated. Heaving breaths tore through my lungs. I was spent.

Were we any closer to victory?

We had to be. Cannon fire had died. The final ships in the air had just met a watery grave. We were winning. *We were winning*. Soon, this battle would be over. Soon, we could go back home. We had already lost so much to these pirates, in the distant past and not one month ago.

Hope gave me a final rush of energy, and I managed to distract our combatants long enough for Bay to serve two a lethal blow. The final man watched his companions fall and ran before Bay had the chance to lay the final attack.

"All right?" he asked me, pressing his back to mine and heaving a breath.

"All right," I confirmed, zoning out of the close

combat and back into the full picture. People on both sides dropped like moths. My vision skewed, but I shook my head and pulled myself back together.

"You've lost your touch, Pan!" Hook's voice sounded above the ringing metal and my ringing head. "I'll give you one last chance. Tell me where the Fountain is!"

"Why would a codfish want to live in a Fountain?" Peter jested, but the strain in his voice was terrifying. Blood, golden as the sun at midday, streamed down his leg.

30TH NOVEMBER

My gut flopped over, and horror struck my chest. My body moved before I could breathe.

Disgust, hatred, fury, it all corrupted Hook's face as he dealt a single, powerful blow. "Fine!" he spat, spittle spraying from his lips. "To hell with you!"

Peter's dagger flew out of his hand with pristine clarity, landing upright in the scarred ground feet away. Golden blood painted Hook's blade as it impaled him. He plucked the weapon from Peter's body fluidly.

Peter, my father, my family, gaped, falling to the cold ground. Tinkerbell's scream shattered the silence ringing in my head as I reached him moments too late.

His lips parted, he stared upwards, unfocused. I lifted him into my lap, feeling the rush of blood pour over my skin, hot and wet. "No," I breathed. I blinked fast to keep tears from blurring my vision.

I couldn't— This couldn't— No. *No.*

Hey, Lyric. His voice filled my head, a memory from

long ago playing before my eyes. *You don't ever have to be afraid. You know that, don't you?* I had just woken from a nightmare. Curled in the bows of our tree, I sat with my face buried in a blanket, feeling helpless. Concerned pixies had filled the air, and I had peeked out at them, up at Peter. He had been so big once, and I'd never stopped feeling quite so small. *You're the Daughter of Pan. We're the same, you and I. No matter what, we have faith, and we trust, and we believe.*

His green eyes dulled, but they found me. A tear splashed against his cheek. His lips curved in the final moment, peace overcoming him. When his breath left him, it was not an ultimate battle. He released it like he'd held it for far too long. The sensation of air leaving him filled me, and I screamed, clutching his limp body against my chest. One by one around me, the same sensation repeated, echoing. *Slightly. Nibs. Tootles. Chubs. The Twins.*

All at once, their breaths found each other, left together.

I screamed my throat raw. Bay yelled for me, but his voice was garbled. His form stood above us, fighting Hook away from my father and I. Everything hurt. Everything was gone.

I curled over Peter, listening to Tinkerbell's shrieking sobs mirror my own and grow weaker. This couldn't be happening. It had to be a nightmare. It wasn't. I knew it wasn't. And yet it had to be.

Pain knotted in my chest, fighting for an escape. A bundle of nerves tightened in my back, winding and winding. Something within me burst.

"What on god's earth!" Hook's voice reached my scrambled mind.

My shirt's fabric tore, and my scream silenced as pain held me in its claws; my lips remained parted, gaping. I clutched Peter as something huge and powerful ripped from my body and flapped. *Flapped.* Power surged in my veins, fueled with a distinct thirst for blood. Panting breaths filled me. Rage left me in tides.

Wings. Real, distinct, feathered wings pounded behind me, lifting me to my feet and away from Peter's corpse. Red blanketed my eyes as I pinpointed Hook stumbling away from Bay. Golden blood still stained his cutlass, and I flicked my gaze from it to his wide eyes.

"You," I hissed, splaying my black wings fully. "What have you done?"

Men rushed at me in an effort to protect their captain, but I didn't have to move a muscle. I stalked forward, and a whirlwind surrounded my body, shredding their skin and tossing them away like trash. I shook. Every part of me shook. The air around me trembled, and a horrible thought overcame me.

What if there *wasn't* air around him?

Lifting my hand, I clenched a fist around the air in Hook's very lungs. I watched as his mouth fell open, and his cutlass stained with Peter's blood dropped to the damp earth. He grasped at his neck. I sucked oxygen from the cells in his body, one at a time. His lips flapped, exactly like a codfish.

He lifted a wobbling hand, plunging it into his coat pocket. Removing a small metal box, he pressed the single, centered button on it.

Explosions ricocheted around me, shaking the ground beneath my feet. I lost hold of my magic, and air pooled back over him. He gasped, sputtering. I spun, spreading my wings to stabilize myself. Blasts of light hit nearly every pixie oak I could see, splitting the trunks.

All of the mainland, all of Aire, and every island connected to it by a bridge fell.

The explosions continued on, and I watched the other large islands fall as we dropped out of the sky.

"If I'm not mistaken," Hook coughed, rubbing his throat, "not all of you can fly."

I growled at him; how dare he? The ground ripped out from under me, and I didn't have time to give him another damn. He was right. All around me, my people were heading toward their deaths. My wings pumped, carrying me over the plummeting islands. I located the nearest path off, then I dove over the edge.

Wind howled, obeying my will as I lifted my straining arms. I molded the air into a cushion beneath each falling island. My vision spotted, and I gasped as they continued to careen toward the rocking blue waters. I couldn't carry them all. I had to let one go. Swallowing, tears hot on my cheeks, I forfeited the one least likely to have anyone on it right now. My home. Peter's secret hideout. Pouring my energy into making sure the islands with people reached the ocean gently enough to survive, I watched the only world I'd ever known smash into the waves. A glimmering water leaked from beneath the rubble, then dispersed, lost forever in the sea.

All wind that rises must fall.

This had been the plan all along.

He is not as infallible as you might think.

They had known from the start.

This was my nightmare and Peter's long-awaited peace. His war, his time, had passed. His spirit had finally found freedom. No matter how it broke my heart.

I limped, my wings dragging across the ground as I took gasping breaths and stumbled over the battered land, searching for Tinkerbell and Peter. Any pirates had since fled, leaving only the carnage of the war behind.

Blood stained my dragging feathers. Mud matted them down. How could I even begin to care when golden ichor still stuck to my pants? A splash of orange coated with dust gleaming silver in the moonlight caught my eyes, and I swallowed, stopping where I was on the mangled battlefield. People and pixies surrounded him, sobs carrying on the still breeze.

Against his chest, I could just make out a tiny, unmoving form pressed to his unbeating heart. Not a single muscle twitched. I didn't need to check for breath to know Tinkerbell had joined him. I was alone.

Lifting my face to the sky, I bit back the tears pooling in my eyes. I was alone. Utterly alone. Abandoned in a way I couldn't fight. In one I couldn't reason with.

"Wind Song?" Bay's soft voice couldn't draw me from the grief, but I forced myself to find him. He stood several paces away, hesitating, clutching his left hand.

My brows furrowed, and my chest squeezed when I noticed the cloth clamped against his wrist. "W-hat?"

His gaze fell to the same place, and he winced. "I guess you missed that part. Needless to say, I don't think my father forgives me for lying to him."

"He cut off your…your hand?" I choked.

"Jealous that I had two, clearly."

I couldn't take it. Any of it. Wails poured out of my chest, and my wings wrapped around me, hiding me secure from the world. I didn't want anything to do with it anymore. This wasn't right. This wasn't right at all. This couldn't be how adventures ended. We had lost too much. So many people. Peter. *Peter*.

"Hey," Bay whispered, pushing through my fortification with little effort. He kept firm pressure on his wrist but bent to catch my gaze. It was too watery to make out much of anything past the concern in his eyes. "It's okay."

"Nothing's okay!" I spat, gasping air.

His lips parted, but he swallowed, thinking better of whatever he was going to say. "Okay…" he said at last. "Things aren't okay." He pressed his forehead against mine and closed his eyes. "I'm so, so sorry."

I wrapped my arms around him and fell apart. He murmured kind nonsense in my ear and stayed close, promising that's what he would always do. As long as I wanted him, he wouldn't go anywhere.

At that moment, what I wanted was out of reach.

The sun rose on a bleak day over a broken land. I clung to Bay's side as Tiger Lily bound his hand after having seared the wound closed. Her eyes were glassy with tears. Everyone's eyes were. Peter had simply always been there for all of us. Just as he was, eternally.

And now that constant, childish joy and comfort were gone.

The last of the Lost Boys were gone.

Tinkerbell was gone.

My home, gone.

I could do nothing but sit by Bay's makeshift bedside in one of the makeshift homes and curl my wings tight around myself so as not to take up too much room in the cramped space. Whisper sat beside me, similarly coiled, and despite her eternal curiosity, she hadn't said a word about my wings since she'd found me on the field. Her fingers were locked around mine.

"It's a good thing, I'm right-handed." Bay examined his bandaged wrist, no humor touching his voice or expression.

Skye sat on his shoulder, mimicking the tone that had consumed all of Skyla. "Didn't look enough like your father before, I guess?"

"He looks nothing like his father." I crushed Whisper's hand in mine. "Not even a little bit."

Skye glanced at me, then lowered his gaze. "You're right. Sorry."

"I can't believe that bastard got away." Whisper released a pent-up breath. "He can't just get away with this."

"He won't." Bile stung in the back of my throat, making it impossible to swallow yet another lump forming there. "I still have to find my siblings and fix that."

Worry tinted Tiger Lily's gaze. "Great power like this can consume you; it is no different than how the Fountain's power fed on Peter all these years. If you let it take control, it will destroy who you are. You must be careful."

I knew that. I had already nearly fallen into the heady rush of this ability. I had nearly sucked a man's life from him, one cell at a time. No matter what Hook had done, that was cruel. That wasn't who I was, and I would never do it again, not like that.

"If you notice any complications, let me know." Tiger Lily smiled weakly, resting a hand on Bay's shoulder. "I wish we could have met again under brighter times, Bay."

"So do I." He dropped his gaze.

"Thank you for helping him," Skye murmured.

She nodded. "Of course."

My eyes widened briefly, but I wasn't even surprised she could understand the pixies. She had once been Neverland's princess. My heart twisted, and guilt soured the taste in my mouth. Tiger Lily had lived through so much worse than this. Her whole world had crumbled numerous times. And yet, she still found the strength to smile, to raise a child like Whisper, to foster a child like me.

Emotion choked me again, so I released Whisper's hand and stood. "Bay, can we go home? Please?"

His brows lowered with confusion.

"It's still there. In the sky even. I'm tired. I just want to go home, please." My lips trembled, and I couldn't hold back the tears that found their way down my cheeks.

Bay looked at Tiger Lily, standing beside me when she nodded. "Yeah, of course."

I hugged Whisper, who confirmed that she'd be with Adam in his fairytale house in the woods if I needed her. Then I flew beside Bay back up to the Skyla I knew, away from the Skyla that had water to lap its shores instead of air. We tucked ourselves into the woods, silently making our way to his treehouse, where this horrible adventure seemed to have begun in blissful moments of peace.

I held my arms around my waist, walking beside him and watching him float along like he hadn't just lost a hand. Skye dipped in and out of the trees. And for that moment, save for the bandage around his wrist, things were okay.

"Does it hurt?" I asked.

"Like a bitch." He smiled.

I found no strength to return the gesture.

Slowly but surely, his treehouse came into view, still nestled high in the bows of pixie oaks. My heart pinched when I saw it, and I stopped short in the miniature clearing. Bay darted for the balcony, landing at the rail and peering down at me. "Hello," he said. My stomach heated at the look in his eye. "To whom do I owe the pleasure of such a late and unexpected visit?"

My skin tingled, and my lips parted. Mouth dry, I answered, "The Daughter of Pan."

His hair glimmered gold in the afternoon light. Loose, it rested around his shoulders, kissing his cheeks in the sweet breeze. My wings took me to him, but I stopped in the air on the other side of his balcony and hovered there, unmoving.

He ran his gaze over me. “I suppose those are just decoration, huh, Wind Song?”

I squeezed my arm, where the feathers he’d tattooed lingered. “These had to come from somewhere.”

“Guess they did.” He pinned a stray strand of my orange hair behind my ear, brushing my cheek with his fingers. “I’m not sure why you’re here. You know all my secrets now.”

My head shook. “Not all of them.”

“Really?” He searched the canopy. “Which one are you missing?”

It took me a second to remember. “What did the Fountain promise you if you drank from it?”

Surprise widened his hazel eyes. He rubbed his jaw. “Well, an eternity with you.” His voice softened. “But I wasn’t sure if you’d want that, and I wasn’t willing to risk my rocky present with you on it. I’m…really sorry about what I did.”

The world stilled around us. My heart ached to hold him; my mind ached to forget the entire day. What if we could just be, for this moment, and ignore the ones that had led to it? “Stupid…” I whispered, fighting more tears. Moving forward, I kissed him, melting into the heat of his touch, the softness of his lips, and the warmth of the instant where nothing was wrong. If I could, I would have stayed there forever. But I couldn’t. Tomorrow, I had to leave. Tomorrow, I’d set out on an adventure alone, an adventure I knew wouldn’t be like the magical stories Peter had told me. Tomorrow, I’d remember adventures weren’t always about meeting new friends and seeing new places.

But tonight… Tonight, Bay drew me into his home

and called it mine. He curled up with me in his arms and talked like adventures were still wonderful. He murmured about pixies and flying and sirens with golden eyes. He pet my wings, a stupid smile on his face every time my breath held at his touch. He reminded me love hadn't vanished from my life.

We talked.

He helped me laugh, just enough.

And I, maybe a little bit right before falling asleep, believed I'd like to be a part of a future with him.

1ST DECEMBER

"I thought I might find you here." Bay's voice startled me, and I looked over my shoulder, parting my wings to see him past the dark feathers. He landed in the rubble, peering at the collapsed trees and neglected pixies' homes. Before me, almost intact, was the large pixie oak with the flattened space at the top. Memories lived in that space, and they hurt. So much.

"Whisper is nagging me about finding you and making sure you're properly packed. I think she's worried about you heading off on your own." He slid his gaze over my body and the cropped shirt displaying my back, allowing my wings freedom to move. He pursed his lips. "Now, I know you'll be fine, but I'm not thrilled you exist half-naked now. Who knows what exotic guys you'll meet out there?"

"More 'exotic' than someone from Neverland?" I asked.

He shrugged. "Technically native to Skyla."

Skye groaned on his shoulder, rolling his eyes. "If

this is going to get flirty, I'm going to leave like I did last night."

My cheeks heated.

"Nothing happened last night," Bay protested, glaring at Skye.

"Ahuh." The pixie rolled his eyes.

"Her feathers were caught on her shirt. I had to be a gentleman and help!"

Skye snickered. "Which was so graceful with your little stub hand, I'm sure."

"Oh, absolutely." Bay looked at me, smiling when he saw my lips had curved up slightly. "What was I saying again?"

I met him, brushing a straying strand of hair over his ear. "Whisper's going to kill you."

"Right. Because she's worried. And I'm not." He rubbed his neck, and his smile faltered a bit as he dropped his gaze to the ground. "But are you?"

"A little."

"Because off the coast, it's going to be really cold, and your back is wide open to any sneaky cold fronts who want to weasel their way into somewhere they shouldn't be?" He quirked a serious brow, and I chuckled. It was a half-hearted laugh, but his eyes softened in response, none-the-less.

"I'm pretty sure I can manipulate the air around me and create a bubble of heat. Also, wings." They were a portable, fluffable blanket. As we'd found out last night.

His smile turned sly, as though he was remembering the same thing. "Whisper is really going to kill me if we don't get moving."

I looked back at the distressed state of my former

home and gripped my satchel. I had so little left of Peter now. Hook had stolen my knife, which I would get back soon, but aside from that, it was just memories and my pan flute. I slipped my fingers into my bag and touched the wooden instrument. "Tell her I'll be there in a moment."

"Okay." He lifted into the air, pausing before going too far. "I love you."

Tears pooled with those words. He'd said them to me so many times last night, but they never lost their force. Taking a deep breath, I whispered, "I love you, too."

Silently, he returned to the now-grounded Aire, and I drew out my pan flute.

The warm notes filled the breeze, and I let tears rush down my cheeks as I played homage to Peter Pan. His name would forever be legend. I would never forget him. With every passing generation, I would teach them all the things he had taught me. Belief is never weakness. Hope is never foolish. Love is never wrong.

Even if all such things could be twisted and tainted, faith and trust were gifts worth giving. In the right hands, and with the right magic, they would almost always let you fly.

"You're only bringing one change of clothes?" Whisper folded her arms and peered at me. "Are you only going to be gone for a day?"

"I can only hold one change in my bag. Besides, food is more important."

Adam stood beside Whisper, doing his best to

remain behind her wrath. Worry coursed through her gaze, spinning in it like a hurricane. "You better not trust every stranger you meet."

"Yeah, I don't need another boyfriend."

Bay snickered, a giant moth perched on his finger. "I second that sentiment."

Whisper shot daggers at him. "You better be on your best behavior while she's gone. I still haven't decided whether or not I'm going to forgive you."

"Come now. I thought the plan was we'd have sass-castic babies together." He delivered the moth to a flower and drifted over to us lazily. "Is now a good time to tell you Tiger Lily invited me over for dinner? I'm going to be helping reconstruct Skyla, starting with your mom's house. I take atonement very seriously, and we really need to catch up." He was lying upside down in the air, grinning ear to ear.

"Skye, you may want to move. I'm about to punch the pixie dust off his smug little face." Whisper shook a fist.

Skye wordlessly bowed and flitted to my shoulder, gesturing for Whisper to proceed. Bay mumbled something about traitorous swine. My heart squeezed. I didn't want to leave this behind.

Taking a shaky breath, and remembering one final thing I had to take care of before I left, I reached into my bag and drew out the vial of Fountain water. It gleamed in the sunlight, and I bit my lip.

Everyone focused on it, but I faced Bay. "Here. For Wendy."

His brows furrowed, and he shook his head. "Keep it. I'll wait until you're back safe, then we can both greet my mom together. She's better than my dad." He drifted right side up, raised a hand, and crossed his heart with his wrist. "Promise."

"But…" I looked at the vial. "This is what you've been searching for, for years."

"Yeah. Pretty great incentive for you to come back as quickly as you can after saving the world. I know there's a great big wonderful playground of adventures out there, but you're not allowed to forget to pick me up before going on them."

"The boy's got a point." Whisper folded her arms. "Even if we're going to be apart for a little bit, you aren't allowed to abandon me. We're going to have our adventures like we always planned."

"But it's all we'll ever have." I asked, "What if I lose it?"

Bay and Whisper both cupped a hand over the water. "Don't."

I glanced at Adam, who smiled and shrugged. "Sounds like solid advice, but I'm just the fourth wing in your little trio."

Skye coughed, loudly.

"A fifth wing, then." Whisper chuckled, kissing his cheek. Sighing, a touch of sadness polluted her smile. She raised a pinky. "I'm going to miss you."

"I'll be back soon." *I hoped.* Linking my finger with hers, I exhaled. Her forehead met mine, and I whispered, "Even now, we will never be apart." Not in spirit. Not ever.

She smiled, but her voice wobbled with emotion. "I'll be right here when you get back."

When we finally pulled apart, Bay asked, "May I fly you to the shore?"

Nodding, I hugged Whisper goodbye and set out with Bay across the sky, toward The Vale's borders; they seemed so much closer now.

"Are you sure you don't want the Fountain water for your mom now?" I asked when we had gone a little ways. "I trust you with it."

"I know. Thank you." He lifted his bandaged wrist and pressed his lips together. "But I still feel like I need to fix things. Tiger Lily was okay in the end, but that doesn't change what I did, the chance I took. I'm going to make sure Skyla's rebuild has at least a dent in it while you're gone. I'm going to make sure Tiger Lily is taken care of, and her daughter knows I'm sorry. Then, when you're back, and I feel I can stand before my mom as a son she can be proud of, I'll wake her with you."

My chest swelled, and I reached for his hand. "Have I told you that I've forgiven you yet? Everything was okay in the end, and you came through in the moments when it mattered the most."

He squeezed my fingers. "You forgive too easily, Wind Song, just like my mom. I'm not going to put my sins behind me as easily as my dad did. I want to be better than him for you."

Airwoman, I loved him. I stopped in the sky and pulled him closer to me, wrapping my wings around his body. Skye zipped out of the cocoon the second before I kissed Bay. "I'm glad you fell out of the sky for me, Star Boy," I murmured against his lips.

He circled his arms around me, not hiding his injury

like his father always had a habit of doing. They both knew where they had lost their hands. One deserved the burden of shame and guilt; the other didn't have that weight to bear. He whispered, "Come back to me safely, Wind Song."

We parted ways after that, my heart full and beating soundly with a mix of anxiety and faith. I could handle anything that stood in my way if I knew it stood between me and getting back to Bay and Whisper, Skye and Tiger Lily, Skyla and Neverland.

I perhaps wasn't prepared for the group of people I saw on The Vale's beach shortly after I left the air above Skyla. They were all around my age, and—worse—magic clung to them so strongly I could feel it like a magnet, tugging me their way.

One of the girls, a dark-haired woman with striking blue eyes, pointed at me, waving me down. I tucked my wings and landed a short distance from them.

Neither of us needed to ask who the other was even though none of us looked particularly alike. A ring of gold circled all of our irises. My breath held, and I didn't know where to begin. All I knew was that this was the beginning……of the end.

A NOTE FROM THE AUTHOR

The Kingdom of Fairytales authors hope you enjoyed this new way of reading. We don't think that a series has ever been set with one chapter a day thought a whole year before and we hope we did it justice.

With this in mind, please leave a review, but when you do, remember that these books were always meant to be short breaks in your day and the blurb reflects that.

We would LOVE it if you can drop us a few words on Amazon

Review here

AFTER THE HAPPILY EVER AFTER...

There is more to these stories. You want to know what happens next right? Fast forward eighteen years...

Pick up book one now

PREQUEL

SLEEPING BEAUTY

1. Queen of Dragons
2. Heiress of Embers
3. Throne of Fury
4. Goddess of Flames

LITTLE MERMAID

5. Queen of Mermaids
6. Heiress of the Sea
7. Throne of Change
8. Goddess of Water

RED RIDING HOOD

9. King of Wolves
10. Heir of the Curse
11. Throne of Night
12. God of Shifters

RAPUNZEL

13. King of Devotion
14. Heir of Thorns
15. Throne of Enchantment
16. God of Loyalty

RUMPELSTILTSKIN

17. Queen of Unicorns
18. Heiress of Gold
19. Throne of Sacrifice
20. Goddess of Loss

BEAUTY AND THE BEAST

21. King of Beasts
22. Heir of Beauty
23. Throne of Betrayal
24. God of Illusion

ALADDIN

25. Queen of the Sun
26. Heiress of Shadows
27. Throne of the Phoenix
28. Goddess of Fire

CINDERELLA

29. Queen of Song
30. Heiress of Melody

31. Throne of Symphony
32. Goddess of Harmony

ALICE IN WONDERLAND

33. Queen of Clockwork
34. Heiress of Delusion
35. Throne of Cards
36. Goddess of Hearts

WIZARD OF OZ

37. King of Traitors
38. Heir of Fugitives
39. Throne of Emeralds
40. God of Storms

SNOW WHITE

41. Queen of Reflections
42. Heiress of Mirrors
43. Throne of Wands
44. Goddess of Magic

PETER PAN

45. Queen of Skies
46. Heiress of Stars
47. Throne of Feathers
48. Goddess of Air

URBIS

49. Kingdom of Royalty
50. Kingdom of Power
51. Kingdom of Fairytales
52. Kingdom of Ever After

JOIN US

Would you like to get Bay's adventure logs? Click the link below to pick your free gift up.

Kingdom of Fairytales FREE gift

Check the Kingdom of Fairytales website for competitions, news and info on all the books and authors

Kingdom of Fairytales Website

Or Join us on our Kingdom of Fairytales Facebook page for fun, games and author takeovers

Still want more? Completely immerse yourself in the Kingdom of Fairytales experience and pick up exclusive offers and gifts

Become a Patron

THE KINGDOM OF FAIRYTALES TEAM

These books would not be written without a great many people. Here is our team:

Many thanks to those who have made this possible.

Thank you to Rhi Parkes without whom, this series would never have come about.

Thanks to all the authors.

J.A. Armitage, Audrey Rich, B. Kristen Mcmichael, Emma Savant, Jennifer Ellision, Scarlett Kol, R. Castro, Margo Ryerkerk, Zara Quentin, Laura Greenwood and Anne Stryker

Also thank you to our amazing Beta team

Nadine Peterse-Vrijhof, Diane Major, Kalli Bunch and Stephanie Pittser.

Thanks to our Proof Reader

Tina Merritt

Thank you to our Patrons

Gigi Nickerson, Amanda Hurst & Coralee Butterfield

ABOUT J.A. ARMITAGE

J.A lives in a total fantasy world (because reality is boring right?) When she's not writing all the crazy fun in her head, she can be found eating cake, designing pretty pictures and hanging upside down from the tallest climbing frame in the local playground while her children look on in embarrassment. She's travelled the world working as everything from a banana picker in Australia to a Pantomime clown, has climbed to the top of Mount Kilimanjaro and the bottom of the Grand Canyon and once gave birth to a surrogate baby for a friend of hers.

She spends way too much time gossiping on facebook and if you want to be part of her Reading Army, where you'll get lots of freebies, exclusive sneak peeks and super secret sales, join up here

https://www.subscribepage.com/v7o8k4

Somehow she finds time to write.

ABOUT ANNE STRYKER

Anne Stryker was born and raised deep in the concrete garden of Jacksonville, Florida. As a Fantasy Romance author, Anne loves crafting fantastical worlds with swoony, humorous, or mysterious male leads and relatable main characters. Embracing the normal in the abnormal is her favorite pastime.

If you'd like to join her in her quest for Happily Ever Afters, you can find her on Instagram or you can join her Faerie Kaleidoscope by signing up to her mailing list:

Instagram: @AuthorAnneStryk
Faerie Kaleidoscope: http://eepurl.com/dGKJ6L

Printed in Great Britain
by Amazon

31644999R00079